Frenzy

James O. Causey

Frenzy

For information and contact visit our website at:
IndoEuropeanPublishing.com

The present edition is a revised version of an earlier publication of this work, produced in the current edition with completely new, easy to read format, and is set and proofread by Alfred Aghajanian for Indo-European Publishing.

Cover Design by Indo-European Design Team

ISBN: 978-1-60444-447-6

IndoEuropean
Publishing.com
Los Angeles, CA, USA

I

For a moment I sat fighting for breath, watching Robin cross the dance floor with that lilting pelvic swing that made you want to cry.

Then, shivering, I downed my drink. It tasted like water. The bartender hovered over me, nervously.

"Please, Norm. It's after eight."

"Shut up," I said, staring across the quiet splendor of the Arbor Room. Robin was mounting the band dais. She stood sheathed in black satin smiling at the patrons—the way she had smiled at me just now. Her voice still shuddered inside me like music, aching and sweet: "He knows, darling. I think he's going to kill you."

The quartet hit a grinding blue note like thunder. Robin began to sing.

She had a kind of magic. It was in the way her voice crept through the air like a mood, like a dream; the way people slowly set down their drinks to listen. She began moving her hips, trying to dance, and the black satin gown impeded her like a halter. She frowned as the drumbeats faded to a whisper, then smiled savagely as she ripped the satin from hem to waist. Her legs flashed free while the drums beat in your brain and the audience screamed.

"Nice, Norm?"

Ingrahm sat next to me, smiling. He was a frail man with eyes like wounds and a beautiful silver toupee.

"Too nice for me, is that it?" I asked bitterly.

"You mustn't drink on duty." His voice was velvet. "It's an off night, the customers want action."

Ingrahm never got excited, never raised his voice. He was soft-spoken, as befitted an emperor. His empire included the Aladdin Club. It included Robin. And me. I sat crucifying him with my eyes, feeling the hatred bubble inside me like lava. He said, "You've been indiscreet, but we'll talk about it later. Go find a table."

It was the way he said it, that remote smile. I went.

I walked numbly past the bar through the swinging glass doors and across the parking lot to the casino. It was almost nine and about half of the thirty tables were occupied. The house girls threaded their efficient way among the tables, collecting chips for the next half-hour of play. Garth Anders, the casino chief, was marking game openings on the blackboard. He smiled hello. Garth was a small blond man, nervous and quick. He had worn that same friendly smile last week when he fired a cashier for being fifty cents short in her night's tally.

I selected a lowball table, five-dollar limit, ten after the draw. A house girl sold me chips. Prom the adjoining table Angelo Ventresca nodded, his pock-marked face impassive. As Ingrahm's number-one errand boy, Angelo rarely shilled.

Angelo was a very special type. I had met men like him at Santa Anita, Las Vegas and Del Mar. Wherever the money flows easily, you see men like Angelo. They are invariably big men, but they move with the lithe grace of a featherweight. It's as if nature was experimenting with the survival possibilities of Neanderthals in a jungle of concrete and steel. A nimbus of violence hovers about them. Their eyes usually give them away. Angelo's eyes were dark and as hard as obsidian; he had the unwinking gaze of a carnivore.

For a time I played in a kind of sick fury, wondering how Ingrahm had found out about Robin. Last night Ingrahm had been out of town. Robin's last show was at midnight. Afterward, she had gone straight home, and I'd phoned her ten minutes later. I'd gone to her apartment at one-thirty and crept out at dawn. No one had seen me enter or leave. How had he found out?

It didn't matter. What mattered now was that I would be punished. Ingrahm was not the kind of man who relished being cuckolded—at women or at cards.

Two years ago I had stalked into the Aladdin shabby and dirty, with the grime of a boxcar on my jeans and six dollars in my pocket. It took the house boys until closing time that night to find out that

2

their new customer was methodically thumbnailing the aces on each clean deck. By then I was five hundred dollars richer. When I left, Angelo chastised me severely in an alley. Ingrahm subsequently offered me a job.

Gardena is a strange town. An obscure loophole in the California statutes permits draw poker and lowball, while banning stud, blackjack, and other variations. In this town, poker is big business— a respectable big business that builds schools and libraries to placate the reformers.

Even the house shills are honest. We spot the grifters, the pros who work in teams, and politely show them to the door. Normally we gravitate to the games that are dying of anemia and do our job there with accomplished artistry. Whether it's a tired aircraft worker or a shrill, bargain-hunting housewife, we can, with a glance or a smile, prod raw nerves to a shrieking frenzy of getting even, hands clutching at the cards, while smiling blondes come by every half-hour to bleed the victim for a quarter.

The Aladdin closed at four in the morning. I cashed in my chips, looking around for-Angelo and Garth. They were gone.

Suddenly I was afraid.

My duplex was five blocks from the club, on a quiet side street. I pulled the convertible into my driveway, hurried up the steps, fumbled with my door keys—and stood frozen, listening to the rustle from the opposite side of the porch.

I turned and saw them. My guts turned to ice.

They stood in the darkness, smoking. Angelo and Garth. The ape and the scorpion.

"This is a lady killer," Angelo said. "This is a pretty boy."

"Nothing personal." Garth's smile was almost friendly as he moved forward.

"Look," I whispered. "Let's not be kids—"

Angelo chopped a big paw into my groin and I doubled over, trying to scream.

3

They did a quick professional job. Groin, ribs and kidneys. It was over in two minutes. They left me retching on the porch steps, tasting blood.

In my circle there are various types of beatings. This was not the kind that left you with ruined kidneys and a broken soul. This was the casual cruelty a Pomeranian would receive for defiling the carpet. Tomorrow I would go to the club as usual. Ingrahm would nod politely and that would be that. Except that I would not speak to Robin again, ever.

I lay there hurting, sick with hate, and then there was the scrape of footsteps on the graveled walk.

"Up, Norm."

The voice was distant, amused. The hands under my armpits were gentle. I staggered to my feet. He was a stocky little man with sad blue eyes and a pouting mouth. His name was Art Mallory. He was a cop.

"Nice job," he said admiringly.

"Why didn't you do something?" My ribs felt broken. I could hardly breathe.

"They didn't need any help."

"You gumshoe bastard."

As I opened the front door, Mallory's pout grew into a smirk. "I told them what you were up to last night. An anonymous phone call this afternoon. Nothing personal." He chuckled.

I turned the lights on and fell across the gray leather couch. I cursed him weakly as he crossed to the sideboard and calmly poured himself Haig on the rocks. He had enough decency to hand me the bottle.

"Why? Why?" I kept repeating.

"So you'd be bitter. So you'd set him up."

4

I almost dropped the bottle. Mallory's blue gaze was sleepy, toadlike.

"Ostensibly, Norm Sands, you're a shill. He pays you one-fifty a week to keep the customers interested. Rather high for a shill. So sometimes you run errands for him. Two weeks ago, for instance. You and Angelo went fishing off Point Fermin. You contacted a live bait boat near the breakwater."

I spilled Scotch on the shaggy green carpeting.

A harsh voice began to make gobbling sounds, and Mallory said, "Don't make me vomit. I don't want a two-bit grifter. I want Ingrahm. Do we deal?"

I said yes.

"I'm just a local cop," Mallory mused. "You make a pinch on a poker-palace employee, you got to have the nuts. Or you're through. I'm too old to pound a beat, Norm." He said it patiently, as if to an idiot child. "You understand? Within the week you're setting him up. With two kilos of horse."

He had left me back at the far turn. I blinked and he wearily explained. "Heroin. Coming in from La Paz, usually by boat. First a trickle of marijuana, now Heroin. The FBI is working with the Mexican authorities on this one. And we've promised to tie it up nice and quiet. Because the reform crowd is beating the election drums this year. All they need is a dope scandal in connection with a club owner to blow the lid off the garbage can. We nail Ingrahm, hell tell us his backers. The syndicate gentlemen who got him the Aladdin franchise. You're going to finger him, Norm."

"Two kilos." I was stunned.

"Just the beginning. Three days ago they caught a distributor in La Paz. He talked. The syndicate is using Ingrahm for their front man on the coast. He's scared, wants to pull out. They won't let him."

"They wouldn't send me for—"

"You make all his pickups. Besides," he said nastily, "you'd think it was tea. For San Pedro High School kids. Well?"

5

I promised to play ball. Mallory said fine.

He paused for a moment, then went on. His knuckles gripping the glass were polished bone. "My next-door neighbor. Name of Johansen. Nice guy. We picked up his daughter the other night at a reefer pad. She's sixteen. She's two months pregnant and can't remember who the father is."

His hand blurred. Ice cubes slashed into my face.

"I've got a daughter myself, Norm. See you."

He walked out I sat watching the ice cubes ruin my carpeting.

I got up and slowly washed Mallory's glass, putting it back into the sideboard. I walked into the bedroom. The face that stared at me from the bureau mirror was a furtive face, with haunted eyes, an ashamed grin. My unfinished letter was there in the portable typewriter on the bureau. I gazed abstractedly at it:

Dear Matt —

Twelve years and I've written twice. I'm sorry, little brother. Still going steady with Laurie? How's little old Mason Flats? I'm doing fine, by the way. Own a half-interest in a night spot, just the beginning. This Gardena's the town I've been looking for. Right next to Hollywood —bright lights and easy money ...

I was trying to finish the letter when panic hit me. It came in a surge of adrenalin-stabbed nerves and stammered obscenities as I tore the letter up and flung it into the waste-basket, threw open the bureau drawers and started packing.

It was dawn. By sundown I could be in another state, in Las Vegas. I could be packed and ready when the bank opened at ten. Hell, I had five hours!

I made myself walk calmly into the kitchen. I brewed coffee, drank it scalding and black, and tried to add up the percentages.

Item: Ingrahm was through, regardless. With or without my help, they would get him.

6

Item: Mallory had me cold. And you can't run far with only six hundred dollars in your bank account.

Item: I wanted Robin.

My ribs throbbed horribly and that was what finally decided me. In his own way, Mallory was a very smart man.

II

I got up late that afternoon and could not eat a thing. I drew a hot bath and lay in the tub for an hour with my eyes closed, retrospecting dully. How does a man become a two-bit grifter? To begin with, he gets orphaned at five, when his parents are killed in an automobile crash. No self-pity, Norman Sands. Some orphans grow up to become bank presidents.

And don't blame it on Aunt Ruby. Aunt Ruby tried. She tried with her raw, red laundress hands, and sometimes she tried with tears.

We lived in a five-room frame house on Orange Street, and there was the insurance, and Aunt Ruby took in washing, and so we got by. I was a dark child, moody like my old man, Aunt Ruby said. Matt was a year younger, big and blond, with a shy smile. People liked Matt. He was an honor student, and the best basketball player in Mason Flats High.

Aunt Ruby had an obsession that Matt should be a lawyer. The summer after Pearl Harbor I got an evening job setting pins in Hermann's bowling alley. Some of the money I made helped put Matt through a summer extension course so that he was able to skip the ninth grade. Aunt Ruby was ecstatic the night Matt told her he had been elected president of the freshman class. "Isn't it wonderful, Norm?" she'd asked me.

I just grinned. A fixed grin. It got so that later the grin would not come off, even when I wanted to cry.

That year I didn't give much of a damn about school, and got lousy grades. The fierce protectiveness I used to feel for Matt had now vanished. Matt didn't need me any more. He was now shooting for a scholarship. I was shooting pool in Hermann's back room. I felt restless, moody. I ran with a fast tough crowd that picked gang fights with the Mexican kids. I began to get a reputation for wildness. After a while people started calling me "that other Sands kid," which made it worse.

When I was in the eleventh grade I fell in love with Laurie Flagg.

Laurie was lovely, a madonna. She had hair the color of a leaping flame, and she was as exquisite as a porcelain figurine. I used to dream about her, breathless sixteen-year-old dreams, full of Stardust and glory.

Laurie was Hal Karse's steady. Big handsome Hal whose father owned an insurance agency. Hal who drove a sharp convertible, peeled and decked, with Carson top and chrome headers. All the girls were crazy about Hal.

Once Hal had been with me on a gang fight in the Mexican quarter. Kid stuff, slingshots and rocks. But Hal had used a broken beer bottle and scarred one Mexican boy for life.

Suddenly Laurie stopped going with Hal. They weren't speaking any more. I would see Hal at Hermann's on Saturday night, brooding over a snooker table. The junior prom was coming up, and now it was Laurie and Matt. You saw them together everywhere; at lunch period, and after school. The whole class talked about it. I felt envious, and yet glad for Matt. Hal walked alone, proud and bitter.

You read in the papers about teen-age violence, about rat-packs and brutal, senseless killings. But sometimes you forget how it really was—the volcanic jealousy of adolescence, the killing fury that can erupt on the school grounds or in an alley after gym period.

On prom day Hal picked a fight with Matt. Matt kicked hell out of him.

All afternoon I worried about it. I knew Hal. But when I tried to warn Matt after school, he shrugged.

That night I was setting pins at Hermann's, and thinking wistfully about Laurie, when Hal came in with Claude Younger and Tommy

Larkin. Claude weighed two hundred pounds and was the best tackle in Mason Flats High. Tommy had been expelled the month before.

They came in flushed and excited, their eyes feverishly bright, their laughter too loud. They had been drinking. Once, between the thunder of the pins, I heard them mention Matt's name. That was when they saw me and their laughter turned furtive.

Something cold came over me. I slipped quietly out the back way.

When I got home the house was dark and still. Aunt Ruby was snoring in her bedroom. I went into our room. Matt lay on the bed, his shoulders shaking.

"How come you're not at the prom?" I turned the light on.

"Go away."

He was a mess. Smashed lips, black eye, and his new blue suit in bloody tatters. He had scrimped to buy that suit. His body kept twitching in quiet agony.

"Hal?" I asked, whispering.

He nodded. I turned the light off.

All the way back to Hermann's I could feel that grin freezing my jaw muscles.

I found Hal's convertible parked in front of Flagg's bar and grill, near an alley just down from Hermann's. The chrome glistened against the black lacquer finish. Hal was very proud of that car.

I really did a job on it.

First, I started on the upholstery with my pocketknife. Working quietly in the darkness, I ruined the dash panel and slashed the padded top to shreds. I poured dirt in the crank-case. In the alley I found a brick and came back to smash the windshield. Then I looked up and saw them.

Claude and Tommy had me hemmed in from the alley.

9

Hal stood in the street, staring at his car, at the thing which had once been his car. He made a sobbing sound, then came at me in a bull's rush.

They hit me together, all three of them. Claude got me by the neck and wrestled me across the walk toward the alley. Hal got hold of my hair and pulled my head back. His fist drove into my face three times and the white street light gushed bloody red. I kept trying to free my right hand from Tommy's grasp, to use that brick.

I bit Tommy's wrist and he grunted, and for a moment my left hand was free to claw at Claude's eyes. His grasp slackened and I twisted, my back arched like a cat's, my face in the gutter.

Then my right hand came free. That brick swung like a flail. It hit Claude alongside the head and he dropped. Hal let go of me and scuttled sideways like a crab, begging. The brick caught him right between the eyes.

I stood up, panting. Tommy screamed and fled down the alley. I started after him, but somebody had me by the arm.

Men were boiling out of Flagg's bar. Somebody was shaking Claude. He sat up whimpering, rubbing his head. Jonas Flagg was bending over Hal. He stared up at me and said quietly, "He's dead, son."

Dead.

The word hit me like a grenade. I felt nausea and a blinding panic. The man holding me stretched his head for a look and I kicked him in the kneecap. He swore, then I was around him and down the alley.

Six blocks later I had shaken them. Darting down the dark streets and through the alleys, shaking with terror. By now they would be at home, waiting for me. The cops would be there, and Aunt Ruby would be crying. It was eleven o'clock. At eleven-thirty the freight made a junction whistle stop.

When that freight pulled out of Mason Flats at eleven-thirty, I was huddled in a forward gondola, shivering. A killer at sixteen, running away in the night.

You learn fast at sixteen. It doesn't take you long to learn about degenerates, about filth, about hunger. You learn about sadistic brakemen, fond of crippling hobos. You learn survival.

At eighteen you are hustling in a west Los Angeles poolroom. At twenty you graduate to floating crap games. You have good reflexes and a natural talent for cheating at cards.

You celebrate your twenty-first birthday by having an eardrum punctured to avoid the peacetime draft. You hang around the tracks in season—Del Mar, Hollypark, Santa Anita. Grifting. A dollar here, a dollar there. Your friends are con men, pimps, thieves.

When you are twenty-five, you drift to Vegas. You get a job dealing blackjack at one of those fantastic luxury hotels. You see how the other half lives, the sleek, richly-tanned men with their women and their good clothes and their Lincolns, down from La Jolla for the weekend. You get so the envy is a knife twisting in your guts.

At twenty-five you're a pilot fish, a scavenger. And you want desperately to become a killer shark.

So one night you decide to score. You plant a ringer at your table and deal him six thousand dollars' worth of blackjacks.

And the house finds out.

And the fingers of your right hand never heal quite straight again.

After that you are reconciled to being a grifter. You shill for Ingrahm, and finally graduate to picking up parcels of Heroin for him.

There are women. Bored, sex-starved housewives who hang around the casino looking for excitement. Some of them are good for a Catalina weekend.

Then one night, you see Robin Page. She is lovely. She reminds you of Laurie. You want her terribly, and this is dangerous. She belongs to Ingrahm. But you don't give a damn.

I stepped out of the bathtub, inspecting the welts along my ribs and kidneys. There was a sour taste in my mouth. Someday I would learn that a pilot fish cannot afford to want anything too badly.

An hour later I went down to the Aladdin. I was drinking coffee in the casino lounge when Ingrahm called me into his office. He asked me how I felt. I said lousy.

"An object lesson," he said dryly. "Stay away from her. Incidentally, I may need you Monday night." Monday was my night off.

"At the Casino?"

"Curious?" He looked at me out of his pale eyes. For the first time I saw him as a shriveling scarecrow, pitifully vulnerable where his sex life was concerned, worried about his toupee, and about his forced role as distributor for the stuff that dreams are made of.

I said no.

"Perhaps," Ingrahm said, "you're wondering why I didn't fire you?"

He wanted me to look contrite, interested. I did.

"You're a very functional tool, Norm. A tool gets broken, you fix it. You're fixed. Aren't you, Norm?"

I said yes.

He made me crawl for a few more minutes and finally dismissed me. Someday I was going to yank that toupee off his scalp, blow my nose on it, then grin at him.

It was a bad night at the table. I lost too many players. At eleven I went into the lounge for coffee and saw Angelo.

"About last night—" he began.

"Nothing personal," I said.

"Good." He looked at me with respect.

"What's with Monday night? A coast run?"

He shrugged and I didn't press it.

As I went back to a table I felt suddenly exhilarated, hopped up. All my life I had scrambled frantically for that quick kill, that one big break. All my life I had failed. But part of getting a break is knowing one when you see one.

I found a seat at a five-and-ten table. It was a tense, quiet affair with only four players. When my deal came, I snuffled the cards a little longer than necessary. After the player on my right cut, my fingers covered the deck for a fraction of a second before I commenced dealing. When I picked up my hand, I held three aces.

Five and ten draw goes fast, and by midnight it had become one of those no-holds-barred games with side bets on high spade and cashing chips over the table instead of calling the house girls for more ammunition. By one o'clock I had salted over five hundred dollars.

That was when I left the game for a while. Casually I went outside, walked across the parking lot to the alley entrance to the Arbor Room, entered and strode on down the hallway and into Robin's dressing room. She whirled from the dressing table.

"Norm, are you crazy?'

"I had to see you."

"Darling, he's taking me home in five minutes. Please—"

I kissed her. She was stiff in my arms for a moment, then all at once her long body relaxed and she began to cry.

"Oh my poor darling, I've been so scared, so miserable. He hurt me. Did he tell your*

I phrased the lie carefully. "He's going to destroy you by degrees. Little by little. He bragged about it last night."

"Oh God."

"It's good-bye, honey. I'm leaving for Vegas Monday night. He doesn't know."

She stood motionless, the idea seeping in. I added, gently, "With a few thousand of his. He'll never miss it. I've got connections in Vegas. The manager of the Flamingo wants me for his new casino boss. It's a break, baby. I'll miss you."

Slowly she pushed me at arm's length. Her eyes got large and dark. It was a moment of revelation, of sickness. She was not quite thirty. Her magic was fading. She had never landed that spot at Ciro's, or the Paramount contract that Ingrahm had promised. In a little while she would be just another singer working for scale in a second-rate night spot and sleeping with the owner, as required.

"Norm," she said faintly. "Darling. Please take me with you. I love you."

I kissed her. I played it straight. I told her they were begging for talent like hers in Vegas, that she would take them by storm. I could see it clearly as an end game in chess, our gradual drifting apart as passion died, as, ultimately, we each came to grips with the incredible selfishness of the other. But now I wanted her.

We planned our departure carefully. Young lovers fleeing in the night. Robin's eyes were wet and shining. She kept telling me how much she loved me.

I went back to the casino and played until closing time. By then I was twelve hundred dollars ahead. I managed to salt most of it and only cashed two hundred in chips at the cashier's window.

I remember whistling as I pulled into my driveway at four-thirty in the morning, and how the whistle died when I saw Mallory sitting on my porch steps like some bland but deadly Buddha.

"For God's sake, suppose somebody sees you?"

"Nervous?" he said sardonically. Without sound he asked the question.

"Nothing definite," I answered. "Not yet."

"Sure?"

"On my mother's grave."

14

"You never had a mother, Norm." He tossed his cigarette butt at my shoes and got up, yawning. "See you tomorrow night."

I stared after him. I was shaking.

III

Sunday was a big day at the Aladdin.

I went in at noon and chose a five-and-ten lowball table. I did not leave that game for twelve straight hours, not even to go to the bathroom. By midnight I had won almost two thousand dollars.

My prime pigeon was a gaunt, tanned man in rumpled tweeds with a diamond stickpin in his tie. After I had hooked him for a hundred, he played in a broken sort of frenzy, staring viciously at my mounting stack of blues. Once I cashed a check for him and that was fine because the hardest part was not in winning but in converting those blues into cash, keeping my stack from growing too large. Our house girls had sharp eyes.

Shortly after midnight I saw Garth, marking game openings on the blackboard. He was signaling at me. I took a slow, deep breath and excused myself, heading for the men's room. A moment later Garth came in.

"Tomorrow night," he said. "A coast run. You and me."

"My car?"

I made it sound casual, unconcerned, though I was feeling the perspiration between my fingers.

"You're not sore about last night?"

"No hard feelings," I shrugged. "You step out of line, you get clipped. Say, I think there's a ringer at my table. That tweedy character playing oil baron. I'm going to take him."

"None of that," he said sternly. "If he's pulling cute stuff, ask him to leave. If he's on the square, he's entitled to the courtesy of the house. You've been here long enough to know that."

Garth was astonishingly moral at times.

By closing time I had won almost three thousand dollars. Driving home I felt strong, ruthless, invincible. I kept trying to recall that line from Shakespeare about a tide in the affairs of man.

Mallory knocked on the door fifteen minutes after I got home. I let him in and mixed him a drink. "Tomorrow night," I said. "We'll probably leave from the casino. I'll be driving a gray Olds convertible."

"That's not enough. Where—"

"I haven't the faintest idea, sorry. You'll have to tail us from the club. Catch Garth flagrante delicto."

"We catch both of you," he said. "You're going to turn state's evidence."

"Not a chance," I snapped. He blinked. "Listen, the minute that happens I'm a dead man, and you know it In or out of jail, they'll get me. Once you catch Garth in the act, he'll sing like a nightingale. But I flit. If you don't like it, you can haul me in right now. Well?"

His teeth bared in a mirthless smile, a fat man's grin. "I tried to tell them," he said softly. "I pleaded with the commissioner. But the poor cautious slob wanted to make sure. Play it safe, make a deal." Mallory sighed. "You don't know how lucky you are, mister. If we'd only had a little more information..."

The hate in his eyes shook me. It was the frozen bitterness of an honest cop who has to deal with filth, and despises himself for it.

"Don't lose the Olds," I said.

Garth and I left the Aladdin at nine-thirty on Monday night I drove, and they turned on all the green lights for us until Highway 101. A light fog was rolling in from the Pacific and I kept squinting into the rearview mirror.

16

"Jumpy?" he asked.

"I'm paid to be."

His tight smile.

We were halfway to Balboa beach when he said, "Pull over. We're being tailed."

We waited while cars hissed by in the fog. I couldn't breathe. It was like dying. "My mistake," Garth said, and I swore at him.

The place was two miles east of Balboa, a deserted stretch of beach cliff with an ancient boat landing in the cove below.

We sat chain-smoking for an hour, and a soft rain began to fall.

Finally Garth cut the lights on and off, twice. He took a flashlight from the glove compartment, said sweetly, "Watch the highway, baby," and got out of the car.

The yellow arc of his flashlight receded slowly down the cliff path. Once the light winked out and there were only the breakers clawing the landing in a silver-crested roar of foam. Then, above the slap of the waves and the drumming of the rain on the canvas top, I heard the throb of the motor launch.

I cut on my parking lamps and eased the Olds in reverse back to the highway cutoff. Two squad cars were there, parked on the apron of the cutoff, glistening in the rain. A spotlight blinded me. I made frantic gestures and the spotlight vanished. The door of the lead car opened and Mallory jumped out. He hurried toward the Olds and I pointed down to the cliff path. He nodded, beckoning me past. His pale face was filled with contempt.

At the highway junction I stopped for a traffic signal and peered back through the dark curtain of rain. One squad car had reached the cliff. Dim figures were emerging. A spotlight flared. I shoved the accelerator down to the floorboard, and the tires sang.

I was doing sixty before I shifted into high. As I hit the dark stretch into Balboa, the faint rattle of gunfire echoed in the wind.

It took me an hour to drive back to Gardena. I drove quickly on the long highway reaches and slowly through the beach towns. I felt as if my brain had become an efficient analogue computer clicking out each move with cold precision.

It was midnight when I wheeled into my duplex driveway. Seven minutes later I had both suitcases in the luggage trunk. At twelve-thirty I coasted to a stop in front of Robin's apartment, scanning the dark streets for Ingrahm's blue Cadillac. No danger. He would still be at the Aladdin, biting his fingernails and waiting. I sat for a moment, reviewing my assets. The Olds. Four thousand dollars in my wallet. Robin.

I was whistling as I went upstairs and knocked on Robin's door.

She opened the door and said, "Come in, darling." I took one look at her face and turned to run.

Angelo leaped out from behind her and hit me alongside the temple, and the hall carpet careened up into my face.

He dragged me inside and shut the door. I weighed a hundred and eighty, but he handled me as if I were a child. From the sofa Ingrahm said, "Where's Garth?"

Robin was sitting next to him, trying to smile. "Please," she said. "They just got here, darling. I didn't—"

Ingrahm gave her a weary glance and she stopped talking.

"He's at the club." My mouth felt dry. "I dropped him off at the club."

Angelo cradled the phone in one huge fist. He dialed. I took a deep breath to scream and Angelo broke my nose with a kick that did not travel over ten inches.

For a moment there was only blackness, shot with yellow spears of pain. From a far distance I heard violins soaring and it came to me that Ingrahm had turned on the radio. Angelo was talking quietly into the phone. Now he was hanging up. He was talking to Ingrahm.

"Cops," he said, and there was a curious dullness in his voice that made me want to vomit. "At the casino. They got warrants for us."

18

He bent over me. "Where's Garth?" he said.

Robin was hunched forward on the sofa, biting her fist and crying.

"Don't blame her." Ingrahm looked old, tired. "One of the house girls reported you two hours ago. We examined the decks you used this afternoon."

Angelo took my wallet. He tossed it to Ingrahm who opened it and sat for a moment, very still. Then he went over to the radio. The sound of violins filled the room.

Angelo started in on me.

Angelo was a craftsman and a specialist in his field. He probably knew more about the location of certain nerve centers than most doctors. It took him about ten minutes to break me, and I told him about Mallory, about everything.

Ingrahm was talking to Robin. He talked in a low, patient voice about staying in Mexico until things could be straightened out. He was very calm. He gave her money and talked about plane tickets. She kept biting her fist and nodding. When they took me outside, she did not look at me.

They herded me downstairs to the Olds. The rain had started again and my teeth were chattering. Angelo shoved me into the rear seat and gave my car keys to Ingrahm.

Ingrahm talked as he drove. He said there was not much time. He said I reminded him of a tomcat he used to have before it was castrated. He did not sound angry, only tired and defeated.

I took a slow, grinding breath and sat up straight. Angelo turned quickly and I mumbled, "Cigarette?" He handed me the pack and a book of matches.

We were passing a switch yard on the edge of town. There was the iron groaning of the freights and the junction lights twinkling crimson as Ingrahm slowed down at the crossing.

I stuck a cigarette in my mouth and fumbled with the matches, holding the heads together. As they flared, I ground that bright little inferno into Angelo's eyes.

He shrieked and clawed at his face. I dived across the front seat, pulling at the door handle as Ingrahm fought the wheel and struck at me; then the door flew open and I was rolling down the embankment.

For a moment I lay in the darkness, tasting track cinders. Abruptly, the blind, yellow eye of the locomotive limned me. I lurched upright and stumbled on along the ties. Twenty feet above, the Olds had stopped. Ingrahm was carefully picking his way down the embankment. Something gleamed in his hand. The freight was picking up speed, roaring. I ran to meet it.

Ingrahm fired three times. He had a bad target and the freight's glare blinded him. I jumped across the track just before the locomotive ground past, pistons snarling. I had maybe thirty seconds. On the opposite side of the track Ingrahm was waiting.

A gondola came by and I grabbed the iron ladder and held on. I climbed with my eyes closed.

Two gondolas back there was an empty refrigerator car with the door half-open. I squeezed inside and found two hobos who swore with hostile relief when they discovered I was not a brakeman.

"Pally," one said, "that door wants to be closed."

"So close it." I was done, finished. If Ingrahm had appeared at that moment, I could not have moved.

One of them lit a match and stared at my face. "My God," he said.

"An accident, pally?" the other asked.

"Argument with a brakie," I mumbled.

You could feel them melt. I belonged.

IV

Those next few months I really hit rock bottom. At night, shivering in a hobo jungle or cattle car, I would dream about getting a stake

20

and heading for Vegas. Only it was February, March, and the California winters are warm, and panhandling was so easy. You had gotten the purple heart in Korea, and it was a loan, buddy, just a loan.

The muscatel helped, too. It helped me forget that I was a piece of decayed flotsam gradually drifting down the sewer. A grifter's prime asset is nerve, and Angelo had broken mine. Then one night they arrested me for vagrancy in San Bernardino—ten days. I had time to take a long merciless look at the beaten wino that had been Norman Sands.

A castrated tomcat! I went quietly mad and bloodied my knuckles against the cell bars. But there was a way to get that stake. The idea scared me, and I tried to forget it. But somehow, after that, I kept drifting down, closer to the flax farms deep in the border southland.

They found me in May, in a rear gondola where I'd tried to hide, and the hard-luck-veteran stuff didn't go. When my feet quit stinging from hitting the dirt and my throat was raw from calling them all the sons-of-bitches I could think of, I looked around. It was the outskirts of one of those jerkwater towns near the border. Sunlight glittered on tin-roofed shacks. Down the tracks, Mexican kids were playing follow-the-leader. Somehow the scene was ominously familiar, part of a half-remembered dream.

Then I saw the sign. It came at me like a fist.

MASON FLATS
Pop. 9,318

I stumbled along the ties. As I passed the Mexican kids, they stopped laughing and stared at me. I walked faster, feeling a dull sickness inside, shivering. A murderer always returns to the scene of his crime.

On my left, sun-baked flats shimmered in the noon haze. On my right, there were tired cornfields and straggling little truck farms. A half-mile down the tracks, I saw the rig.

It was about fifty feet high, on the cleared edge of a cornfield. The

21

rotary engine throbbed deeply to the whine of the cable drum. Two drillers in tin hats were arguing by the silver storage tank.

My chuckle had a harsh, flat sound. Ever since I could remember, small outfits had drilled wildcats here, small outfits with oil fever that invariably hit salt water and sand.

A few hundred yards later, I cut across a weed-grown lot and walked down the lane of clapboard shacks that was Orange Street. In twelve years the houses had grown older, poorer. A dying street in an aging town. I turned up an alley.

Center Street. Old man Hermann was mopping the sidewalk in front of his bowling alley. He looked yellow and old, his cheeks mottled with liver spots. He peered sharply at me as I passed and suddenly I felt naked, as if everyone on the street was staring at me.

Once I would have died rather than let Matt see me ragged and dirty, with my shoes falling apart. But that stake was becoming an obsession.

I passed the alley where I had killed Hal. There was Flagg's bar and grill. Next to it was a two-by-four stucco office with a sign in the window: Matthew Sands, Licensed Real Estate Broker.

Matt had wanted to be a lawyer so badly.

I took a deep breath and walked into the bar.

Darkness after the sunlight. The warm, quiet smell of sawdust and stale beer. The bar was deserted except for a big blond man who was polishing the bar and whistling. He gave me a little-boy frown.

"Draw one," I said.

He hadn't changed much in twelve years. He still had those football shoulders and puzzled blue eyes. As he scraped the foam off the glass, he paused, looking at my shoes.

"One dime, mister."

"I'd think it would be on the house."

"All right now, that'll be ten cents."

His mouth got hard and I chuckled. "Okay, Matt. But I'd sure buy a long-lost brother a drink if—"

"Norm," he burst out. Beer foamed on the counter. "Norm! I'll be utterly damned." He reached across the bar and almost broke my shoulders in a bear grip.

"Ouch, you big bastard, don't spill my beer."

"Beer, hell," he said, reaching for the bonded sour mash. "How come you didn't write, let somebody know?"

And it was good, sitting there drinking with him, the way it had been fourteen years ago when we had both had our first drink out behind the garage and gotten sick together. Matt talked about it. He talked about how Aunt Ruby had died; about his two years in Korea; about quitting law school when Laurie's father had a stroke, and running the bar for her; about his real estate business and how he and Laurie were finally getting married next month. It was good until he stopped talking and began to stare at my clothes, at my three-day-old beard. But there was no pity in his eyes. If there had been, as much as I needed a stake, I would have turned around and walked out of his life forever. But his look held only bewilderment.

"What in hell happened to you?"

"Business reverses," I said wryly. "Look, I need three hundred bucks. If you haven't got it, I need two hundred. You'll get it back next month, promise."

"If that's all you want," he said, hurt. "I was hoping you'd hole up here awhile, put on twenty pounds."

"Hal. Remember?"

Matt grinned. "Six stitches and a concussion. You couldn't kill Hal with an ax."

It took a moment for his words to sink in. When they did, there was only a queer numbness. I wondered why I did not feel a vast and heady relief. Later, it came to me. You live with a leaden weight on your soul for twelve years, and when the weight is finally lifted, it leaves an indelible scar. I was scarred for life.

23

"How about some breakfast, Norm?"

He looked at me, wistful and full of hope. He had it all figured out I would stay, maybe go into real estate with him, help him tend this fourteen-stool bar. I would be best man at his wedding and some day marry a nice home-town girl and have kids and play bridge with him on Saturday nights while our wives gossiped across the table.

"Some ham and eggs and you'll be a new man." Matt started through the swinging doors of the kitchen. "Oh, Laurie." He almost knocked her down.

"It's Norm," Matt said proudly. "He's staying awhile."

I stared at her and couldn't speak.

Her hair was still the color of flame. Her fine gray eyes slanted imperceptibly at the corners and her lips were full and rich. Under the black turtle-neck sweater her breasts leaped at you, and even through the blue jeans you could see the outline of those long lovely legs. There was nothing in her face, absolutely nothing.

"Fix him some ham and," Matt beamed. "I've got to tend bar."

I followed Laurie back into the kitchen. I felt weak, giddy.

"Over easy all right?" She broke eggs onto the grill, not looking up.

"Fine." I swallowed. "How come you two aren't hitched yet?"

"We've been engaged for six years," Laurie said evenly. "First it was Matt's finishing college. Then the postwar draft. Then Korea. Then college again. Then Papa's stroke—the operation cost three thousand dollars. Then Papa died. Money," she said with an infinite bitterness.

"Lovely word."

"Then," she said, "it was Norm."

We stared at each other. For one fleeting instant I saw in her face something that was like a throbbing volcanic fury, a wild thing at bay. Then it was gone. She brought the eggs over, her face

24

expressionless. The coffee cup rattled in the saucer as she set it down.

"In case you want a bath," she said coolly, "Matt's room is upstairs. First door on your right."

She went into the bar and I stared at the eggs. Two days since I'd had a decent meal and now I couldn't eat. The food choked me. The coffee was acid.

I found Matt's room upstairs, a cramped cubicle with an old army cot and dresser. In the bathroom I discovered a razor, and I kept chuckling as I shaved, crazy giggles of pure delight as I lathered under the steaming shower. In Matt's dresser I found a pair of clean denims and a white shirt. His shoes were a loose fit.

Coming downstairs, I heard them arguing in the kitchen.

"But honey, he'll be a natural in real estate. Norm's a hustler, a go-getter. We'll be partners—"

"Partners!" Her searing contempt made me wince. "We're getting married next month, remember? Then we're selling the bar and moving away from this rotten town like you promised."

"But Sam Peabody called this morning, about the wildcat. They're in showings, black sand at twenty-six hundred! Sam gave me a net listing on the adjoining acre last month. When the well comes in—"

"It won't come in," she said wearily. "Like your big apartment deal last month that fell through on escrow. Like all your pitiful golden schemes that evaporate. For once in your life stop dreaming!"

"Please, honey—"

I started whistling loudly, and came into the kitchen. Laurie looked knives at me and went out to the bar.

"I'll be moving on this afternoon," I blurted out. "Thanks for the clothes."

"Aw, stick around awhile," he said miserably. "Just for this afternoon." He brightened. "You can help me tend bar."

"Why not?" I had blundered into a place where I wasn't wanted, but it didn't really matter. I wasn't staying.

For the next hour, I helped Laurie strew fresh sawdust on the floor. Once she looked at me with a faint smile. "Clothes fit all right?"

"Fine." I wanted to slap her.

A few customers drifted in and I helped Matt serve them. For a Sunday afternoon, business was slow. Laurie went about her duties with a tight-lipped precision, not speaking to either of us. Two men started a game of shuffleboard and Matt told them enthusiastically about Sam Peabody's wildcat, about how Mason Flats was going to be a boom town. It was a good time to sneak out the back door and hop a fast rattler to Bakersfield.

That was when the fat man with the briefcase came in and ordered Scotch and water. I served him, trying not to stare. He was something to stare at.

At first glance you got the impression of a circus freak. The face was a pasty white with full red lips twisted into a perpetual smile. It was a face to pity, to laugh at. Until you saw the eyes. He wore a rumpled gray tropical worsted that bulged over massive shoulders, and he was not fat at all.

"Seventy cents, sir," I said, and he chuckled, moving down the bar toward Matt at the cash register. I started around the bar, fast arid Matt grabbed my arm. His smile was a corroded grimace. "Hello, Mr. Lombard."

"Tom Bullock was here last night," the big man said gently. "With some county officials."

"We appreciated the business." Matt's grin shook.

"He spent forty bucks."

"It was thirty-three-fifty," Matt said stiffly.

"Tom said forty." The fixed clown smile.

Matt slowly took two tens out of the cash register. He handed them

26

over and Lombard said, "The yokels with him spent twenty-eight bucks. Fifty percent comes to fourteen."

A tiny muscle leaped in Matt's jaw. He gave Lombard three fives. The big man handed him a dollar and looked at me with cold amusement. "Who's the punk?"

"His brother," I said, not liking it. "What's the pitch?"

"Better tell him the facts of life, Matt. Incidentally, your Scotch stinks."

Deliberately, he upended his glass. Ice cubes danced on the bar, whiskey splashed on my shirt.

Rage exploded inside me, molten and seething. I grabbed him by the coat lapels, yanking him halfway across the bar. "You small-town hick bastard," I said. My right fist speared him flush in the mouth. He went backwards, arms flailing, and sat down with a spine-jarring thud.

Nobody moved. The men playing shuffleboard stared. And Matt was whispering, "God, Norm, please," and was vaulting over the bar, helping Lombard to his feet, babbling, "I'm awfully sorry. He didn't know."

Lombard pushed him away. He straightened his tie, not looking at me. Then he walked through the swinging doors and Matt said thickly, "Did you have to do that?"

"Who in hell is he?"

"His name's Pete Lombard. He used to be a sadistic vice-squad cop. Now he's Murdoch's hatchet man. Murdoch publishes the Clarion—he owns this town, stock and barrel. Tom Bullock happens to be chief of police. He brings in business, he gets a cut."

I was amazed. "That goes on here? In this jerkwater town?"

Laurie came in from the kitchen and slammed down a jar of pickles on the bar. 'Tell him about our fair city," she said viciously. "Tell him about the red lights on the edge of town, the basement crap games, the graft!" Her lower lip was trembling. "And how they'll shut us down now because your plague of a brother stepped on the wrong toes."

She bit her lip as some customers came in. I watched her serve them beer and mumbled, "You mean that might revoke Laurie's license?"

Matt nodded tiredly. "They'd say we served beer to minors, that we were running a fag joint, anything. One of the city council cousins wants this spot. He offered Laurie two thousand for it last month; she turned him down."

One of the shuffleboard players ordered a hamburger and Laurie brought it out from the kitchen. Now she was talking with him. They were both coming over. Laurie's smile was bright.

"Norm, you're staying awhile, aren't you?"

"Well—"

"It's flax season at the mill and they're taking on temporary help. Norm, meet Hal Karse."

The tall man stared at me. Slowly his hand went to the scar on his forehead. "I'll be damned," he said.

"I know you're too big a man to bear old grudges," she said. "Norm's our guest. He's looking for work."

"I'm just a foreman," Hal said woodenly.

"You drag weight with the super." She touched his hand. "Please, Hal."

He couldn't take his eyes off me.

"You can come around to the grain elevator, six in the morning," Hal mumbled. "If you want."

"You're such a dear," Laurie twinkled.

Hal went back to the shuffleboard and finished his beer. When he left, Matt said, "Gee, that's swell."

28

"You might at least say thanks," Laurie said.

"Thanks," I said.

V

That night I slept in Matt's room. He was very cheerful about the future. Soon Mason Flats would be a big town.

We would prosper together in real estate. Next month I would be best man at his wedding. I finally fell asleep and dreamt about Laurie.

Next morning I went down to the mill at dawn. Hal put me to work bucking hundred-pound sacks of grain onto a conveyor belt. The yard was like an anthill, incoming trucks dumping flax down the scale chutes, Mexicans everywhere, men dragging bags of grain into the storage sheds through a haze of flax dust. A buck-forty an hour. Those Mexicans loved it. Most of them were wetbacks, tramp fruit pickers down from Imperial in the off season, and this was a soft political job, this was wealth.

Hal rotated the other men's jobs, stacking empty bags, shoveling flax into the hoppers, but I stayed behind the conveyor lifting sacks waist-high, an eternity of hundred-pound sacks. Every ten minutes Hal would walk by and say, "Keep them moving."

I mopped sweat from my eyes and sneezed from the flax dust. I thought about Laurie, wanting to kill her. But what the hell had I expected, sucking around where I wasn't wanted, trying to mooch a handout they couldn't afford? I felt very tired.

Nine o'clock and spell time. Men lounged against the loading ramp, lighting cigarettes. I slumped, dead tired.

Hal came over to me, hands on hips. "Spell time only for permanent help. Buck those sacks."

I got up slowly.

"Don't you like your job?"

I tugged at the last sack. It weighed ten tons. Abruptly, my knees gave way and I sprawled across the sacks with the world going round in a fiery pinwheel of sunlight and sweat and dust.

"I guess you're not used to work," Hal said sadly. "Better go get your time."

It was a quarter to ten when I walked into the bar. Laurie was all alone in the kitchen. She looked at me, very pale. "What happened?"

"Hal paid me off for that brick. I just stopped to say goodbye."

Her bright head bent wearily. "I'm sorry. It seemed like a good idea at the time. Today is like one of those old silent flickers; you know, the tragedy scene where everything goes smash. Our liquor license is being revoked. Selling liquor to minors, they say. I called city hall and they just laughed at me." She made a grimace. "Big-businessman Matt is next door, getting blotto. It seems he just lost another million."

"How come?"

"He's not a businessman." Her eyes were brimming. "But he won't admit it; he keeps trying. He was too proud to get married before the justice, he wanted us to go first class, a big white wedding. All his life he's tried to be like you, the big man, the sharpshooter. What's funny?"

"Nothing's funny."

"Good-bye," she said.

"Good-bye, Laurie."

I walked slowly out to the street. Through Matt's office window I could see him slumped over the desk with a bottle. I opened the door.

"What gives?"

He stared up vacantly. There was shiny sweat on his face and his eyes were glazed blue marble. He said, with a terrible effort, "The well just came in. A half-hour ago. Looks like three hundred barrels a day."

"I don't get it! You've got a listing on the adjacent acre—"

"Had," he corrected owlishly. "It was an open listing; I never insisted on an exclusive. Last night one of Murdoch's sharpies talked Peabody into an oil lease. Peabody just called me." He giggled. "I've still got a listing on the lot, exclusive of mineral and petroleum rights. Matt Sands, the big-time operator!"

I looked at him, feeling sorry and ashamed and trying to think of some way to say good-bye. Then I felt that old fierce protectiveness welling up inside me.

You spend twelve long years living by your wits, and you acquire a very specialized education. Any grifter has a good memory, and mine was excellent. It was almost a conditioned reflex, my brain growing as keen as winter starlight, as I was evaluating, remembering a man called Pop Toren.

At least, "Pop Toren" was the name he went by. I had spent a very profitable summer with Pop six years ago at Santa Anita. Pop was a white-haired old gentleman who looked like a saint and happened to be one of the best bunco artists in the business. During the second Huntington Beach boom, he made two million dollars. Pop had taken me under his wing that summer, had taught me certain things.

I said to Matt quietly, "Who knows about the well?"

Drunk as he was, something in my voice made him look up. "Nobody yet." He hiccoughed. "By noon it'll be all over town. Why?"

"What time does the hall of records open?"

"Ten o'clock. Who gives a damn? Hey, come back with that bottle!"

Ten seconds later I was next door, behind the bar. My hands were shaking as I poured certain things into a highball glass. It was a brutal way to sober him up, but there wasn't much time. I ran back into the office and handed Matt the highball glass.

31

"Where's the bottle?" he protested.

"Drink this first. It's good. Real good."

He drank it and promptly vomited. Messy but quick. It took me five more minutes to get him back to the bar kitchen and start pouring black coffee into him. Laurie watched us with listless contempt.

"It won't help," she said. "He'll just get drunk again."

"No he won't. Where's your car?"

Matt was white and twitching, but at least he was sober. "Laurie?" he said helplessly, and she gave him her car keys. I grabbed him by the arm. "Now come on!" I yelled at him.

Her car, an eight-year-old convertible, was parked two doors down. Before we started I made Matt bring along his checkbook and some standard lease forms from the office. He didn't get it. Driving the four blocks to City Hall, I tried to explain, but he kept saying pitifully, "Honest to God, Norm, I've only got ninety bucks in my bank account."

It was one minute past ten when we walked into the Title Records Office. The clerk yawned at us while we pored over the townsite map, then he took an agonizingly long five minutes to thumb through the property-records ledgers. All the time we were jotting down landowners' names and addresses I was scared that somebody else would walk through that door. But nobody did, and it took only ten minutes to find the names I wanted—the names that owned the ten nearest land parcels adjoining the Peabody wildcat.

I had parked the convertible around the side of the building. As we got in, I saw two men hurrying anxiously up the hall steps. One of them carried a briefcase. It was Pete Lombard.

Five minutes later I brought the convertible to a grinding stop on Orange Street. We started for one of those ancient frame houses with a parched front lawn and dirty paint peeling off the front door. I rang the bell. Inside, a baby squalled fitfully. The door opened. The woman wore a faded blue wrapper, and her cowlike eyes were dull with resentment. "We don't want any, mister. You woke the kid."

"We're from Consolidated Oil. Are you Mrs. Cashin?"

She stared dumbly. Her lips parted. Suddenly she wheeled and fled back through the house. "Ma. The well come in!"

I took Matt firmly by the arm and steered him into the parlor. The furniture was a dusty, faded velour, the rug was threadbare. A God Bless Our Home needle point hung over the mantel. From the depths of the house the baby's squalls rose to a shrill crescendo, and stopped. It had either died or gotten its bottle.

Mrs. Cashin and daughter finally came into the parlor.

"Here they are, Ma," the daughter said reverently. "They're from Consolidated Oil. Isn't that what you said, Mister?"

"That's correct." I beamed at Mrs. Cashin. She was one of those shriveled grandmother types with sharp black eyes —the kind that love to ask questions. I had to gamble on the windfall approach and pray that she didn't ask for our credentials.

I cleared my throat. "Mrs. Cashin, you own the half-acre parcel north of Peabody's, right?"

"That's right," she said, and I relaxed. Her voice was quavering and eager. This was going to be easy. "Is it a big well?" she asked.

"Thirty barrels a day," I shrugged. For a moment I thought she was going to cry.

"However, Mrs. Cashin, our company has authorized a dozen leases on property within a half-mile radius of the well. Yours happens to be the last lease. You'll get standard landowner's royalty, naturally."

Mother and daughter looked at each other and smiled.

It went off perfectly. I filled in two lease forms granting Mrs. Cashin one-eighth landowner's interest and giving Norman Sands, agent, exclusive mineral and petroleum rights. Mrs. Cashin read the lease twice, pursing her lips. She finally started to sign when the daughter said nervously, "Ma, don't you think we ought to wait for—"

"Of course," I interrupted smoothly, "you'll get a thousand-dollar advance against royalties. Give me the checkbook, Matt."

He handed it over. He was lost, a man in a dream.

I wrote Mrs. Cashin a check for one thousand dollars, and hesitated. She eyed the check hungrily.

"Our chief geologist says your parcel doesn't lie along the fault line," I said carelessly. "Apex and Standard Oil think we're crazy, but Consolidated likes to gamble. Of course, if you'd rather wait for another company to contact you..."

She signed. I had her daughter sign as witness. They were both smiling at that check as I pushed Matt out the door.

"You idiot!" Matt blazed. "I don't have a thousand dollars in the bank."

"I signed the check, little brother."

He kept shaking his head. I wanted to explain, but we had nine more places to hit and our path would very shortly intersect that of Pete Lombard and friend. When that happened, we were finished.

But I took a few minutes, anyway, and talked patiently and earnestly until Matt got it. His face was rapt with something akin to adoration. Then he frowned. "But supposing you can't redeem those checks today?"

"Then I go to jail. Where in hell is Larkspur Street?"

It was on the west end of town and we wasted ten precious minutes finding the address. Wasted, because this particular landowner was not at home. I kept punching his doorbell and swearing. Then I had a chilling thought.

Suppose Mrs. Cashin scurried right down to the bank and deposited that check. But she wouldn't. It was human nature to gloat, to flaunt that check in front of the neighbors. I seemed to hear Pop Toren's voice, mild and soothing. "It's the oldest swindle in the world, son. But if they're got oil fever, it always works."

Two hours later we were shaking hands with a hayseed named John Tolliver, congratulating him on his lease. Out of eight landowners, we had managed to sign three people to leases. Two of the eight

34

hadn't been at home and the other three had already heard about the well and wanted to consult their lawyers before doing anything rash. I had written three rubber checks for one thousand dollars apiece.

As we started to drive away from Tolliver's house, a black Packard sedan ground to a stop in the driveway. Lombard jumped out, followed by a hawk-featured little man. They hurried up the porch steps and rang the bell.

Presently the front door opened. Lombard and friend expostulated with Tolliver while I lit a cigarette and blew smoke rings. Now Lombard was shouting. The front door closed in his face. He turned, saw us.

"Hi," I waved cheerfully. "Gobbling up leases today, gentlemen?"

Lombard started down the walk fast, and the little man grabbed his arm and whispered something. Lombard nodded. They came up the walk.

"You didn't waste much time," the little man said, trying to smile.

"You got to skim off the cream afore the flies come," I said in a nasal twang. "Mister Murdoch's going to be right unhappy, isn't he?"

It jolted them. Matt got out the duplicate leases and showed them to Lombard. He grunted. "Pretty rough, huh, Ted?"

"But legal," Matt said.

Ted squinted at the leases. He looked at me, at the battered convertible. "I see you paid through the nose for these." His smile turned dreamy.

"Might you be interested in selling?"

"You catch on quick," Matt said, overplaying it.

"Did you pay cash for these, friend? Or issue the good old bouncing check?"

I managed to look blank, but Matt flinched. Ted pounced like a cat.

35

"It's an oldie, friend. Nice try, though. You'll probably get off with eighteen months."

"I don't know what you're talking about," Matt said, white. I could have killed him.

"Like hell you don't," Lombard said, getting it. He grinned. "Tell you what, fellows. You sign these leases over to us and we'll see those checks you wrote are honored. Otherwise—"

They were fast. Fast and rough. But I still had one final hole card. "The checks happen to be good," I said softly, "but we still want to sell. Directly to Murdoch."

They hated the sound of that name. Their glances crossed. "He'll flay you," Ted said.

"Possibly. But when he finds out how you boys botched this little caper, I wouldn't give much for your chances either."

"You're bluffing."

"Can you afford to call?"

They couldn't. They withdrew and argued for a while in angry whispers. Then they came back and started haggling.

It was almost closing time when we walked into the bank. Matt kept staring at that check as I endorsed it and handed it to the teller. The check was for five thousand dollars, made out to one Norman Sands.

"Two thousand in clear profit," Matt breathed. "Not bad for four hours' work."

I wanted to hit him, but what was the use? "If you hadn't given it away, it would have been ten times that," I said. "Hey, look."

It was Mrs. Cashin, standing in line at the cashier's window. Matt licked his lips. "Pretty close."

"Life is a gamble, little brother."

Driving back to the bar, Matt kept chattering happily. Within a week there would be five thousand hungry strangers standing on each other's shoulders for breathing space in Mason Flats. The boom was here, and we were getting in on the ground floor. We were both going to be filthy rich. When he finally ran down, I broke it to him as gently as possible.

"One grand apiece," I said. "Fifty-fifty. It's enough for you and Laurie to move away, to get married on. Tonight I'm leaving for Vegas."

"Gosh, I thought we were going to be partners and—"

"Listen," I said brutally, "and try to understand. You've got no talent. You'll never have it, not if you live to be ninety. I can't afford to stay here and wet-nurse you the rest of your life. Get an honest job somewhere, you'll be happier."

I coasted to a stop in front of the bar. Matt sat forlorn, crushed, looking at his hands. After a long moment he said quietly, "At least come on in, have a drink. Say good-bye to Laurie."

I didn't want to see Laurie again. But I followed him into the bar and had a drink while Matt told her about the whole deal. As he talked, Laurie's eyes got that strange primitive intensity again. She stared at me, and now the intensity was stronger, almost frightening.

"Congratulations," she said. "Are you still leaving?"

It was the way she said it, the taut smile, her breasts thrusting defiantly against the black sweater. My mouth felt dry. All right, I thought, you tried to fight it. At least you tried.

"No," I said. Matt looked up, eagerly.

"Damn, that's swell!" He was radiant. "Tomorrow we'll open up a decent office downtown. Oil securities, acreage! Look, I may not be the smartest guy in the world, but I can learn. You'll see."

Laurie's eyes still held mine, but now the mockery was fading, slowly being replaced by fear.

"Sure," I said. "You'll learn."

VI

Our office was on Main, across the street from the Clarion building.

At first Matt howled about the two-hundred-monthly rental. Six weeks later he spent a thousand dollars on carpeting and a flagstone planter framing the front window.

We ran splashy ads in the Clarion: Sands Realty. Land. Oil. Leases. Securities. Come in, you lucky ground floor speculators. Get rich!

They came. Some of them were Matt's friends, Laurie's friends. A queer frenzy attacks people during an oil boom, a mad compulsion to draw out their life savings and give them to the first broker who promises a fifty-percent return. I promised a hundred percent. We had a map on our office wall where I pointed out gusher sites to prospective investors. In those first two months the population of Mason Flats tripled. A city of tents and trailers mushroomed on the edge of the flats. Everywhere the drillers—drunk, their jeans spattered with oil—were spending. Giving their money to the girls in the back room, to the smiling cold-eyed boys in the basement keno parlors.

That first month we grossed three thousand dollars.

Laurie used to stop by our office daily. She loved to catch Matt in the middle of closing a deal and beg him to take her to lunch. They would usually be gone half the afternoon. When they returned, Laurie would be wearing that cool, possessive smile, and the needle she seemed to have for me would be out and ready.

"How're the parasites doing today?"

"Very funny," I would say inanely, wanting to penetrate that brittle smile, to hurt her. By now our antagonism was a naked sword. Matt never noticed. He had a virginal innocence about such things.

After the first two months, Matt began to get squeamish about our prosperity.

"Fifteen hundred, kid," I'd point out to him. "A good day's take, what?"

He had a white pinched look. "I feel like a skunk, Norm. All my friends went into that Cormont lease. The sure-fire gusher, remember?"

I remembered. The Cormont development had come in salt water and sand. "All investments are gambles, little brother."

"Laurie wants me to quit. She says these securities aren't worth a plugged nickel. That it's the same as stealing."

I stared at him. His eyes slid away from mine. "You want to quit, Matt?"

"No."

Matt was finally learning. Matt, with his new twisted smile. He drank too much. He drank far too much the night Laurie gave him back her ring.

"Forget about her, kid. Let's go to Amy's. She's got some new girls, a blonde six feet tall. Real fine, just like a step-ladder. Come on."

"Go away."

"You goddamn jellyfish! You promised her you'd quit working with me and she still wouldn't say yes, no, or go to hell. She's not worth it. Give me that bottle and come on!"

He came.

The following night I was working late, setting up our weekend ads, when Laurie stomped into the office and put her hands fiat on the desk and her face six inches from mine and said, "Where is he?"

I reached into the sandalwood box on my desk and took out a dollar Havana. I lit it, taking plenty of time. I flicked imaginary lint from the sleeve of my two-hundred-dollar imported Oxford flannel, all the while smiling at her and savoring it. Laurie's breasts rose tremulously with her breathing.

Then I picked up the phone and dialed. "Amy?" I said. "Norm. Matt sober yet? Fine. He'll probably make a two-day party of it. That's right," I said, looking at Laurie. "He likes redheads. Soften him up with redheads and send me the bill."

I hung up. Laurie sat unsteadily, her eyes never leaving my face. She had lovely legs. "I deserved that," she whispered.

"You got it."

"All right," She was listless. "So we're even now. Let him go, Norm. Please."

"Listen," I said patiently. "Within a few months we'll be out of business." Hope flared in her eyes, then slowly died as I went on talking.

"In the first place," I said, "the boom's leveling off. People are getting smart, demanding solid leases. It's not my fault your friends won't talk to you any more because they were dumb enough to make some bad investments. But if it'll make you feel better, I've got an option on a proven quarter-acre. We're drilling. When the well comes in, I'll pay your friends back, dollar for dollar. Fair enough?"

"No!" she wasn't buying it, any of it. "Do you know what you're doing to Matt?"

"I'm making him rich, that's what I'm doing to him. And you're glad."

"Glad?"

I stood up. My tongue felt thick, swollen. "Because now you don't have to feel sorry for him any more. He's found something bigger, and it galls you." I came around the desk toward her. "You never did love him and were ashamed to admit it."

"It's me," I said, "isn't it?"

She stared up at me. She was trembling, visibly. Her gray eyes were wide and frightened. I was standing near the wall switch. I felt hollow, all cold inside. I reached out and turned the lights off.

"Norm—"

I took her by the shoulders. She stood up easily, her face a pale blur

40

in the darkness. I could hear her breathing. I reached out and she melted into my arms.

For just one moment it was all right. Her lips were hot and wet and she made a small moaning sound. Then, suddenly, she was crying. She tore free, and her hand slashed across my mouth.

"Damn you," she sobbed wildly. "Damn you, Norm."

The office door slammed behind her. I touched my lip, tasting blood.

The following month our business got a little dirtier, a little more shabby around the edges. We made money. It had become an obsession, to forget about Laurie and make money. I was no longer a pilot fish; I had finally grown my dorsal fins.

One day Pete Lombard came to our office and invited us to join the civic realtor's league. A thousand-dollar membership fee plus five percent of our gross take. 'Tell Murdoch," I said, "that we're not pimps or bookies. We don't have to play ball with the county sheriff and local Johns. Tell him that, clown."

"Don't call me that," he said in a low voice. "Some day you'll slip. Punks like you always slip. Clem says I can have you then. You're going to cry, mister."

I stared at his pink smile, remembering the stories I'd heard —how in his vice-squad days he'd loved to make arrests; how one girl had died of internal hemorrhages shortly after he'd booked her.

"Sure," I said tightly, wanting to smash him like a fat grubworm. "I'll bet you're a big man with the whores. Especially when they're handcuffed and you've got a blackjack. Beat it, clown."

"Some day," he said, and went out.

"They'll wait," Matt said, shaken. "One slip, that's all it takes."

"Relax. These two-bit grifters give me a pain."

The following weekend the Clarion refused to accept our

advertising. It should have worried me. The Sands Brothers had managed to acquire a rather smelly reputation, and business was falling off badly. The bubble was starting to burst. But I didn't give a damn because we were finally drilling our own wildcat, on the south end of the flats.

We had twenty grand by now, in a joint checking account, but Matt seemed strangely reluctant to touch it.

"Keep it for a nest egg," he said. "Get the bank's six percent; you never know when you'll need cash."

Good old cautious Matt. I played along, blind, unaware of the gathering storm.

"We're getting sued," Matt announced one day.

"Huh?"

"Craven. The northwest development that petered out last month. He claims misrepresentation. Wants his money back."

"Tough luck."

"He's suing next week."

I yawned.

"I saw Laurie yesterday," Matt said.

"Oh," I said carefully.

"She's working at City Hall. Records clerk." Something in his voice made me look up.

"Still carrying the torch?"

"No."

But there was a time fuse smoldering in him, and two nights later the bomb went off. It took a white-haired widow with bright eyes and a trusting smile.

"You're sure it's quite safe, Mr. Sands?"

"Solid as the mint, Mrs. Gride," I reassured her. "You're a lucky little lady."

Matt sat quietly watching me take her money. When she left he said, "Very smooth."

"Four hundred bucks."

"The bank called today." His face was wooden. "Their interest was due yesterday."

"So they'll get their interest." I felt very cheerful. "I went out to the well this afternoon. They're in showings finally, good old black sand! Just two more weeks and we'll be sitting on top of the world."

Matt worked very hard that night.

"Hey, those are marks we've already had. Forget them."

"I need this list." He was stubborn-drunk. "I got to have this list."

It happened next day. Matt drew out every penny in our joint account, and vanished. I didn't see him for three whole days. I almost went crazy.

Saturday afternoon he came in and threw a briefcase on my desk.

"Where in hell have you been?"

"Here's your securities back. Your gilt-edged toilet-paper securities."

I just stared.

"I bought it back." There was a holy glare in his eyes. "Every bit I could find. Only the money ran out. Here's a list. We still owe these people."

"My noble little brother," I said.

Then I was on my feet, moving around the desk. "You crazy Galahad, you dumb son of a bitch," I said. I hit him in the mouth. He stood there, blood trickling down his chin; then he turned and walked out. The following Monday he got a job bucking tongs on a pipeline. Fourteen bucks a day. A few nights after that I saw him walking along Center Street, holding hands with Laurie. They were smiling. I walked into the nearest bar and got quietly drunk.

Six weeks later I was flat broke. Everything had been so beautifully timed! The same day the bank clamped down for their interest, crybaby Craven filed suit. The Clarion splashed the suit all over the front page.

That morning I sat staring, numbly, at the paper, at Murdoch's acid editorial. "Unscrupulous bunco artists posing as decent realtors... butter-tongued parasites who prey..."

After a time I threw the paper in the wastebasket and went back to the washroom. I stared at my gray face in the mirror, then took a tranquilizer. Better. Much better. I went back and glared at the phone, waiting for the bank to call. If only they hadn't read the morning paper. If they extended the loan just one more week, I'd be stinking rich. Why didn't they call?

It finally rang. I was shaking so hard I could hardly pick up the receiver.

"Yes, Mr. Cromwell," I said. "No, Mr. Cromwell. Oh now listen, you can't do that. There's a lake of oil just another hundred feet down. Look, if it was that yellow rag's smear story this morning—I'm suing of course—you're crazy," I screamed, my voice raw. "Just another week! I'll give you half-interest! Make you rich as Midas. You got to leave that equipment alone—"

I was mouthing things into a dead wire. I threw the phone at the wall and slumped behind the desk, shivering.

In six months I had come full circle. From rags to riches to bankruptcy.

I sat staring at the unpaid bills on my desk, frantically trying to think of some loophole, some angle. There didn't seem to be any. I was dropping the unpaid bills in the waste-basket when the phone rang again. It was Harker, about the rent. I hung up on him and went outside.

44

Halfway across the street, I stopped. He was a gray, tired little man lounging on the corner, and he had Finance Company written all over him. I kept walking until I hit the street corner, then doubled back up an alley and jumped into my Cadillac.

I drove fast, down Orange Street, toward the edge of the flats. Out there was my well, the Sands Number One, with no men to run it, no money left to pay for the pipe I'd borrowed or the back salary of the drilling crew. The crew was all right. They'd wait another few days. Another three days and it would be a thousand-barrel-a-day well. The bank wouldn't strip the equipment for at least a week. Pipe. I had to have pipe.

I drove across the tracks to the cluster of long galvanized sheds that marked the beginning of the derrick jungle. I went from place to place, sweating and feverish, trying to make them understand about the pipe. Just one week and I'd pay. They laughed. I kept at it all that long, hot, horrible afternoon, but it was no good.

And then finally, through the choking dust, I saw my rig looming up, deserted.

I got out of my car and climbed up onto the derrick platform. I gazed at the next well across the way—its bailer working, its bit smashing through solid rock a thousand feet down, and I wanted to scream. I saw Matt on the other platform. He was bailing, one foot on the sand wheel drum, that sand line shimmering past his sweating face. Suddenly, I wanted that bailer to snag, the cable to cut him in half.

Down by the sump there was a liquid flurry of motion. Oil splashed blackly as two Mexicans writhed in the sump. The four men, who had pushed them in, stood on the bank laughing. The Mexicans stumbled waist-deep through oil and clawed painfully up the bank. A squat brown man in a leather jacket started after them, three big toughs trailing at his heels. The two Mexicans retreated.

"We'll be back, amigo," one said calmly.

"Any time," leather jacket said, hands on hips.

I walked across to the sump. Leather jacket came up, stocky and smiling. "Friends of yours?"

"I work for Murdoch," I said coldly.

He stood motionless as I mounted the platform. Matt gave me one wary glance and bent back to his sand line. "Watch it, that's the line super down there—"

"Those greasers," I said. "What was their pitch?"

"You wouldn't be interested," he said bitterly. "They've got some stupid idea that Mexican roustabouts should make more than six bucks a day. Beat it."

"Sure," I said, and leaped to the ground. I ran over to the Cadillac.

Two minutes later I caught up with the two lean fanatics, who were plodding wearily along the highway. "Need a lift, fellows?"

"We'll manage, gracias."

"Look, I saw what happened back there and it's a damned shame. Get in, it's four miles to town."

The nearest one scratched his long, broken nose reflectively. "We'd mess up your car, amigo."

The fools wouldn't get in so I just cruised along next to them, talking, and presently I felt the old familiar excitement take hold. This was perfect! A hundred yards later they had talked their hearts out. I told them I'd just remembered an appointment, and off I flew in a cloud of dust. They gaped after me. It takes all kinds.

Driving back to town in the blue dusk, I kept thinking about it, smoothing the rough edges. It was one hell of a gamble, but I had absolutely nothing to lose. I parked the car in an alley six blocks away from the office.

The little gray man still dozed in front of the office, sullen because of the waiting. He stuck the repossession notice in my face. "Whereas," he droned, "by default of monthly payments—"

"Thanks, pop. Good night."

He scowled uncertainly. "Where's the car?"

"Loaned it to a friend."

I started to shut the door and he put his foot against the jamb.

"You got a warrant, pop?"

I shut the door in his face and went over to the desk. I wrote until midnight, then plugged in the hot plate and heated a can of beans.

I wrote and rewrote until four in the morning. It was good stuff, but not strong enough. It had to scare them, grab them by the throats. It needed names, incidents.

Next day I did field work. I went from derrick to derrick, cautiously avoiding those I had visited the previous afternoon, telling everybody that I was a reporter from the Clarion. After a couple of hours they got wise and I saw the line super hurrying after me with two roughnecks. I made it to the car just in time.

I pawned my watch that afternoon and went over to the American Legion auditorium. They wanted seventy-five bucks for the hall Saturday night. I started to walk out and they called me back. We dickered and finally they came down to forty for Friday.

Next I went to a printer's shop. When I showed him what I wanted, his eyes popped and he said fifteen bucks instead of five. I didn't haggle, but it left me with exactly eighteen dollars and seven cents, all the money I had in the world.

Now I needed help. I needed help for the filthiest swindle a man ever pulled on his friends.

So I sat down and called Matt.

Then I called Laurie.

VII

"I don't get it, I just don't get it."

"Like I told you, I've changed."

Matt kneaded his big hands painfully, looked at Laurie. "What do you think, honey?"

She looked thoughtfully at the yellow handbills on my desk. "So the wolf grows fleece. Why, Norm?"

"What's in it for me, is that it?"

She picked up one of the posters and began reading: "Dear Mr. Murdoch and Associates:—We, who mine your black gold, we who toil—" Her wry smile came on again. "... Why are we discriminated against? Because we are Mexicans? Because our skin is brown?... The vampire of starvation wages, hazardously rotten working equipment— But that's not quite true, Norm."

"So I want a crowd."

"But what will you—"

"A coat of tar and feathers, that's all I'll get out of it. Murdoch ruined me with his slimy editorial and I'm going to hurt him back, right where it'll hurt the most—his big hairy pocketbook!"

My voice broke off as I stared out the office window. My Caddy was rolling grandly down Main Street. So Mr. Finance Company had finally found it.

"I could have gotten out of town with a whole skin," I said bitterly. "I had to play it dumb. Help the little guy. I asked you here because you two are the only decent people in this town with enough guts to help me. If you don't want in, say so."

Laurie's smile was suddenly breathtaking. "All right, Norm. Your motives are dangerous. But the thing in itself is good."

Matt picked up a batch of handbills, grinning. "She'll hand them out on street corners and I'll cover every rig on the flats. You'll get your crowd."

I said that was fine, and they went out holding hands. Looking after them I felt suddenly sick, unclean. Then I had a horrible thought. Suppose Murdoch ignored the whole thing? Would he? Could he afford to?

48

Next morning I found the eviction notice on the office door. I laughed, picking up my handbills. Either way it wouldn't matter.

All morning I nailed those handbills on fences and telephone poles. That afternoon I canvassed the Mexican quarter. I found a dozen starving wetbacks who were delighted at the prospect of earning a dollar each to play shill. At first they thought I was muy loco, but finally they got it. It was a mere matter of listening to a speech tonight, and clapping the hands.

It was dusk when I knocked on Matt's apartment door. He was just finishing supper. "Laurie's meeting us down there in twenty minutes," he said eagerly. "Had supper yet?"

"Sure." I was starving. "Let's go down to the hall."

When we got there we found a few Mexicans milling about uncertainly in front of the closed doors, and a small reception committee standing on the auditorium steps. Pete Lombard and a cop.

"The party's off, boys," Lombard said gently. "Nice try."

"What's the idea?"

"Give me the injunction, Dave." Lombard took the paper from the cop's hand and purred, "Whereas your use of this hall for inflammatory and libelous speeches is a public nuisance—"

"Public nuisance my fanny," Matt snapped. "You can't keep us out."

The cop drifted forward, one hand on his nightstick. He was a big cop, with a serious, round Irish face. I licked my lips and stared past him at that auditorium door. Behind that door lay money. Money and power. Only I would never get past that door. Murdoch was a thorough man.

"You can't do this!" Matt was shoving Lombard to one side.

"It's a free country—"

The cop's nightstick blurred. Matt crumpled on the steps.

49

"Inciting a riot," Lombard said. "Better take them in, Dave."

They jerked Matt roughly erect and started down the steps. That was when Laurie pushed her way through the gathering crowd and confronted them.

"Where's his gun?" she whispered. Her cheeks were flaming. "Who did he kill?"

"Libelous speeches," the cop said awkwardly. "The law—"

"Damn the law!" The Mexicans watched, quiet brown faces in the dusk. "A man has a speech to make," she cried. "This country isn't free if a man can't speak, can't raise his voice when he sees something evil. They can't shut our mouths with clubs. I'm going in!" Laurie started up the steps. "Hit me!" she shouted at the cop. He stood frozen. "No—I'm a woman. People are watching. Well, there's going to be a speech. And people are going to listen."

She walked, tall and proud, through that door. I followed her. Nobody stopped me. I felt weak, dizzy. The footsteps behind me were many drums beating.

"... Murdoch's got you and you by the throat! Sure, he pays the drillers decent wages. He has to. But you boys are Mexicans. Cheap greaser labor! You're being exploited and you're too gutless to do anything about it. Ugly word, gutless ..."

The swimming sea of brown faces. Laurie, sitting in the front row with Matt, pale and rapt. Lombard leaning against a pillar, looking amused.

"... pay you what they want, dole out accident compensation when they feel like it. Jose Garcia—yes, you—remember your brother Pedro? Sure! We all remember Pedro. I went to school with Pedro. A rusty crown block falls on him, and they call it carelessness! And you there, Juan Mendez—how does it feel to get caught in a sand line backlash and lose an arm? How does it feel when you think about the accident compensation you're not getting, the money that's your rightful due? Look at him, men—but don't pity him. Pity yourselves!"

The applause rocked the rafters. Those shills had been a good investment. Lombard was gone now. I could not see him anywhere. I held up my arms for silence.

"They tried to stop this speech because they're afraid. But you boys are going to organize. We're going to lick Murdoch. We're going to make him install decent working equipment, pay accident compensation, and a fair day's wages!"

The shills started again and the applause rolled. That was the end. Suddenly I was afraid. These boys wanted more than a ten-minute speech. They wanted organization, action.

Thank God, here they came.

They drifted casually through the side doors—big men, quiet and purposeful. Lombard walked down the aisle toward the stage. I could have fallen on my knees with relief.

"You communist son of a bitch!" Lombard yelled.

Heads swiveled, stared.

"Get off the platform, you stinking red!"

"Listen to me, boys," I roared.

Boos and catcalls drowned me out. Then a sudden spurt of movement, hecklers shoving people, overturning chairs. A tomato splashed on the stage curtain behind me. Matt, white-faced, bulled his way toward the thrower. Another tomato came, this one right at me.

A many-throated snarl. The eruption. I leaped into it.

Faces bobbed in front of me, red and angry. I had my back to the stage dais, a chair in my hand. I splintered the chair over heads—it didn't matter which heads. I saw Lombard a few feet away using a leather sap with grinning deliberation.

A careening truck smashed into my face and I went down. Someone was kicking my ribs in. I tried to cry out, and then there was only a spangled darkness.

51

"He's all right. Norm!"

I sat up, wincing. The empty hall was a shambles. Laurie was bending over me. She had a black eye. I tried to grin at her. "What time is it?" I croaked.

"Ten o'clock." Matt's face was a tear-stained mask. "Those bastards."

"No cops?"

"They didn't need cops. Come on, we'll get you to a doctor."

"Murdoch. I got a date with Murdoch. Let go."

Laurie was biting back tears. "Oh, Matt, look at his face.

Go get a doctor, please. Hurry. I'll take him home."

Then, somehow, Matt was gone and Laurie had my arm, was helping me toward the door. Nausea spun blackly in my stomach as we went out into the night. Now Laurie was helping me into a car, her little convertible.

"I'll drive," I said. She handed me the ignition keys.

We sat for a moment in darkness. I was aware of the warm pressure of her thigh against mine. She did not pull away. I stared at her, at the tremulous rise and fall of her breasts, and a thousand jigsaw pieces spun slowly into place. Her petty bitchery, her eagerness to find a cause, her desire to save Matt, to save me. She was one of those women who search desperately for a vision greater than themselves, and right now I was that vision.

I lit a cigarette. I had to see Murdoch. And fast! He had made a tactical blunder, and now it was my move. But it was all gold, this thing I had found, and Murdoch could wait. As I snubbed the cigarette out, Laurie's lips were wide, moistly parted. Twin spots of color glowed in her cheeks.

I kissed her. She did not fight. Her fingertips were moth-wings on my face and her lips were hot and avid. We kept kissing and her breath came wildly in my ear. She was panting something about Matt going for the doctor, and she had to take me home. I laughed.

I flipped on the ignition and drove fast down Main, past the rail junction and the galvanized shacks of Supply Row, and now the speedometer quivered at eighty as we raced past the derrick jungle. My hands were frozen on the steering wheel.

I turned off the road, skidding to a stop in a darkened eucalyptus grove. Laurie shook as I took her in my arms.

"Oh, my darling," she whispered. "When I saw you up on that platform, I really knew. I love you, Norm."

I ran one hand under her dress and she stiffened, her face buried in my shoulder. "Please," she said. "Not this way, Norm. I'm all yours, but please—"

My hands kept moving, and she said faintly, "All right. Whatever you want, dearest."

There was a proud humility in the way she took off her sweater. She was trying not to cry. And it would always be this way between us— anything for Norm, our whole life together.

She looked at me, waiting, and a part of me slowly shriveled and died.

"What is it?"

"Put the sweater back on." My voice sounded strange. I flipped the ignition and gunned the motor. Driving back to town, I didn't say a word. She sat very close to me, murmuring, "Please tell me, Norm. I've failed you, haven't I?"

"Shut up."

She was still.

I turned on Main, and parked in front of the Clarion building. Murdoch would still be in the pressroom writing a vitriolic editorial about the local commie element.

I opened the car door. "Good-bye, Laurie."

"Norm."

"Listen." I took a deep breath and shivered. "I want you to stay away from me. I'm strong poison, do you understand? I slime everything I touch."

"It's not your fault, darling. The union—"

"There won't be any union," I said through my teeth. "Get that through your thick head. It was a gimmick, a crowbar to use on Murdoch, get it?"

My words were steel barbs sinking in, hurting. "Marry Matt," I said. "Marry him soon. And if you happen to see me on the street, turn around and run like hell."

She sat white and stricken. I got out of the car and slammed the door. I walked across the street without looking back.

VIII

The downstairs lobby was deserted except for a colored janitor who goggled as I passed. My face was a devil's mask of dried blood.

I climbed the marble stairs, my ribs aching. On the third floor I limped down the corridor toward the lighted office marked "Clem Murdoch, Publisher." I stood with my hand on the doorknob, frantically trying to remember my pitch, the way I'd rehearsed it a dozen times. The hell with it, I thought, and threw the door open. The talk and the laughter died.

A cone of smoky light hung over the green poker table. Cards and chips stopped rustling. The faces that turned in my direction were blank and hard. Lombard languidly got up from the table and started toward me. He was smiling.

"Peter." The thin, sharp voice came from beyond the cone of light.

Lombard stood motionless as I walked past him and around the poker table. Murdoch sat there, silver-haired and stiffly erect. His eyes held mine. They were frosty blue, derisive.

"You play poker, son?"

"I want to talk to you," I blurted. I fumbled for a cigarette.

Big men sat around that table, the powers of Mason Flats. Fat Sam Kramer, head of the city council. Fat Sam with his soft woman's body, who got a take from those basement crap parlors, a percentage on civic-construction bids. Sam looked at me coldly, then at Murdoch.

Little Tom Bullock, the best chief of police that money could buy, sat next to Kramer. Bullock the middleman, who kept both the county sheriff and the city council darlings happy with rakeoffs from the perfumed brothels on Orange Street.

Bernard Kroll, toying bitterly with his stack of blues. Kroll's construction company was a large thorn in the city council's side. His consistently low paving-contract bids made the construction grafters uneasy. Ultimately, Kroll's honesty would destroy him.

Next to Kroll sat the most beautiful woman I had ever seen. She was blonde and sleek and her smile was catlike. Our glances locked. Her name was Shannon Quinn. I had seen her once at a country-club dance with Murdoch. Rumor had it that she was a thousand-dollar whore Murdoch had imported from Las Vegas.

With an effort I ripped my gaze away from her and looked back at Murdoch. He chuckled and glanced sharply at Kroll. "Like I said, a man who doesn't fold when he's beaten is a plain damn fool. Bernard?"

I was being ignored. Everyone was suddenly looking at Kroll. I got the impression of a silent duel being fought by two titans. Kroll hesitated, his face impassive. He flicked a blue chip across the felt.

Murdoch grinned and shoved a small stack of blues forward. "And five hundred," he said.

Kroll stared at the pot, Indian-faced.

"Look at him." Murdoch's voice hung softly in the haze. "He knows I'm bluffing, but he's afraid. A three-thousand-dollar pot, and he's afraid to risk five bills." He tapped his cards on the green felt. "Tell you what, Bernard. Call me, and I'll add this—and this—" He added ten blues to the pot, then another ten. "Four thousand, five. Bernard?"

Kroll's face knotted with concentration. His eyes darted from the pot to his own scant stack of blues. He squinted at his hands, then at Murdoch's face, and finally tossed his cards into the discard heap.

Murdoch's laughter was like ice crackling. He spread his hand, face up. A soft sigh rippled around the table.

"Just two jacks," Murdoch drawled. "Openers." His voice became very gentle. "Could you have beaten them, Kroll?"

Kroll's smile was bloodless as he reached for the whisky. But it was the girl's face that held me. Her lower lip was full and richly curved with mockery as she refilled Kroll's glass.

"Excuse me, gentlemen." Murdoch got up stiffly. "Take my chair, Peter."

Lombard came forward and Murdoch walked toward the door in back marked "Private." I followed him. My cigarette tasted as bitter as lye.

Some office. A naked light bulb dangled glaringly from the ceiling. A rickety roll-top desk stood by the window, with a great brass cuspidor beside it.

"Don't look so shocked, Norman," Murdoch grunted. "Only the rich can afford to sacrifice show for comfort." He sat in the old leather throne behind the desk. "Sit down."

We measured each other.

His weathered face had a thousand wrinkles. The thin lips were those of a fanatic. The flint jaw properly belonged to a Caesar, a Bonaparte. He was a ruler of men, and power was his obsession. And now he was waiting for me to make my pitch before he laughed in my face and turned me over to Lombard.

I took a deep breath and plunged.

"A yellow handbill," I rasped. "Mexicans unite, one man making a two-bit speech. And right away you get scared, call out the riot squad, rotten tomatoes, clubs. Shall I tell you why you're scared? Because you're a figurehead, someone for the town to hate—"

"Knock it off," he snapped. "The Mexicans don't care. They're wetbacks, they drift like sand. They're paid scale for roustabout labor and you know it. Lombard offered you a chance to join the fold."

"For peanuts!"

"So now you eat hulls."

"Wrong again."

"Lay it on the line, Sands. You've got something to sell."

"Only that I can hurt you."

"You could annoy me." He made a fly-swatting motion. "Nuisance value only."

"How much is nuisance value worth?"

"Ah," he said sardonically, "so you want to work for me?"

"For us. I want you to appoint me Municipal Landowners Agent."

He began laughing. Shrill, spasmodic gasps. I kept talking, outlining my idea.

"The city of Mason Flats owns a hundred-odd acres of tax-delinquent titles—vacated eminent-domain stuff which it farms out to major oil companies. I propose that you, the city council, establish a staff to represent the city as an active corporation, said staffs entire duties to consist of running down oil acreage, buying it in the city's name, sandwich leasing when direct buying is impractical—"

"And you'll be chief agent in this little setup, eh?" He looked thoughtful. "Obviously the city might benefit from this with the proper staff. However...."

"What's in it for Murdoch, huh?"

"Precisely."

"The plums. I could ferret out enough producing acreage to keep the city treasurer happy, and then the hundred-barrel-a-day stuff—"

"Well," he said slowly, "well, well."

He sat, toying with the idea, weighing it. Then he smiled wolfishly. "It's a good idea, Norman. Brilliant. Now I'll tell you what I'm going to do. First, I'll give you twenty-four hours to get out of town. Then I'll have Peter Lombard appointed Municipal Landowners Agent. Thank you for the idea, Norman. Good night."

He waited. I didn't move.

"I'll want ten thousand a year," I said deliberately, "and bonuses. Plus the right to pick my own staff. I'll go see Sam Kramer tomorrow morning."

His eyes bored into me, a cold, joyous tight flickering in them. "If I'd had a son..." His hungry grin flashed on. "Suppose you stay a while, son, and we'll talk about it."

I stayed, and we talked about it.

I found Matt next afternoon, in the derrick jungle. He stood stiff and intent at the humming sand line as I mounted his derrick platform. At first he'd be furious and hurt, but he'd listen to reason. We needed each other; that was the important thing.

The men at the cable drum ignored me. Matt looked up, and his eyes were alive and scared. "The bailer snagged an hour ago ... I can't leave the line. Look, I can loan you a few bucks to stay out of town until this thing blows over."

"You haven't talked to Laurie?"

He shook his head painfully. "She called me late last night. Said she was sick. What happened?" Then he stared past me, to my parked Cadillac. "You got your car back. How come?"

"Murdoch and I made a little deal. We're in!"

His eyes were rapt. "You mean he came through? He'll pay a decent scale to the Mexicans?"

"That's dead. Forget it."

I started explaining about the new job. As I talked, his face grew slack. He stared at me dully.

"Ten grand a year, and bonuses! Don't you get it?"

"I get it," he said. "A lot of guys got their cans beat off last night so you could get a foot in the door." He turned back to the sand line.

"Matt," I said.

"Take your goddamn hands off me."

The two roughnecks watched us. I was getting sore. I grabbed Matt by the shoulder. "Listen, stupid—"

The blow came out of nowhere. It caught me flush on the mouth.

I spun sideways on the oil-slimed planking and landed hard against a joist. Matt stood over me, pale and shaking. "Now beat it," he said thickly. "Stay away from me or I'll kill you. And stay away from Laurie."

I got up, slowly. I feinted, and Matt drove his right fist into my belly. I went down, retching. When I finally got up, Matt's swing was wild. I palmed him hard in the throat. As he slipped, I drove a knee into his groin and he slumped with a moan.

I fell on top of him, beating his head against the platform railing. He managed to wriggle sideways and deliver a short chopping right to the temple that broke my hold. Then he had me in a bear hug over the railing, and I felt my spine give. He came up with his hand and drove that balled fist right into my face. He was sobbing brokenly.

Suddenly he stepped back. I clung to the railing. He was trying to say something.

I stumbled forward and threw my left fist at his chin. He skidded, went down. I aimed a kick at his face.

59

He scrabbled sideways, painfully, and his ankle folded. I lurched after him and the platform reeled beneath my feet. Someone was shouting, "Bailer's snagged. For Christ's sake, duck!"

I stared drunkenly at the sand line. It hung slack, quivering.

Then it backed. It hissed angrily out of the shaft and began to unravel, coil upon coil—twenty feet, thirty, fifty. It was alive. It writhed in hissing coils over the derrick platform, knocking me down.

For one moment I blanked out. When I opened my eyes I was flat on my back, staring at blue chunks of sky through loops of cable, the black crossbeams of the rig. The cable moved. I moved with it, a fly caught in a web of steel.

I clawed madly at the web, and suddenly I was free. The two roughnecks were fumbling with the cable drum, trying to reverse it. Matt was enmeshed in a dozen loops of cable. His face was white. The cable tightened slowly about him as the sand line slithered back into the hole.

I stumbled over to the drum, yelling at the roughnecks to put the cable into forward. I pointed at Matt, and they stared. They got it.

I ran over to Matt's side and tore at him. He had two lengths of cable knotted around his waist and over his shoulder. His lips moved. He was praying.

The cable drum moaned.

From above, the sand line began to drop, slackening ever so slowly. I stumbled blindly about the platform groping for the cable cutters. One of the roughnecks still fought the drum; the other tugged uselessly at Matt's shoulders. I fumbled for the cutters, and all the time my eyes were fixed on that cable sliding like a long, oiled snake into the shaft. I could almost see it before it happened—Matt being dragged, screaming, across the platform, the cable fouling at the shaft in a tangle of flesh and steel.

Finally, I found those cutters. I floundered to Matt's side. My hands kept slipping in the oil. I cut through the first two strands.

There was twenty feet of cable left on the platform, then ten, five. The driller wrapped his hands around that steel rope, trying to keep a half-ton bailer from sinking deeper into the earth. Suddenly he shrieked and stared at his maimed hands, at the flesh which had sloughed away as easily as butter.

There was one strand of cable left. As I ground the cutters into that strand, the cable thrummed taut. Matt slid six feet away. I followed him, but he was being jerked away, faster, toward the mouth of the shaft. I closed my eyes, waiting for his scream as he was torn in half.

Silence. I looked up, numb.

Matt lay still. There was no more cable on the platform. That last strand had parted.

We finally got Matt free. His grin was crooked as he grabbed my shoulder for support. "You sprained my ankle, you bastard."

The two roughnecks helped me get him to the car. It was a miracle; they couldn't believe it. "You both all right?"

"We're fine," I told them. "Go fish for that bailer."

We drove silently through the derricks. My whole body was one tired ache. My face felt bathed in flame. Matt was smiling ridiculously through puffed lips. "You still want me to work for you?"

"We need each other," I said.

"Supposing I pull another double cross?"

I thought about it. "I'll take that chance."

"Fair enough," he said in a strange voice. "Partners."

IX

"But the geologists said—"

"Damn the geologists! I'm telling you the region's all hard-rock shale! Even if there was oil, they couldn't get through with a diamond tit. Look, Mr. Davis, the city needs this new school. We'd hoped to find a few public-spirited citizens who didn't have oil fever, who'd sell their land for a fair price."

"Well, I don't know."

He chewed his little mustache and wiped his horn-rimmed glasses and squinted nervously at me from behind the hotel desk. Every few minutes a roomer would come down the rickety stairs and he would peer sharply at them to see if they were taking any luggage with them.

"Two thousand dollars." I made it sound like two million. "Well?"

His smile was an awful thing to see. "Well, Mr. Sands, I hate to tell you this, but a Fargo Oil scout approached me three days ago. They want to drill. I'm to get standard landowner's interest."

I thumped on the desk and told him the Fargo people were crazy (the bastards), and he was apologetic and frightened, but that's the way it was. Neither of us mentioned the 500-barrel well a thousand yards north of his two acres or how the field had been moving southeast the last few months.

"The city has authorized me to go to twenty-five hundred," I said. "Last offer."

"I think I ought to wait."

"You can't afford to."

His eyes got round and scared. I crossed the lobby and stood at the window, staring through the gilt "Davis Hotel" sign at my Cadillac across the street I lit a cigarette—our prearranged signal. Matt got out of the car.

"Pretty old hotel," I said. "You know the city condemned Schultz's Boardinghouse last week. Terrible eyesore. Fire hazard."

Davis' mouth opened, but no words came. Matt entered, looking big and cruel in his new blue gabardine. "Mr. Davis," I said, "my

62

brother Matt. Matt's with the Public Health and Sanitation Department. You won't mind showing him around."

"Just a routine inspection," Matt said. He frowned darkly at the front door. "This your only exit?"

"Yes, we—"

"Let's look at your fire escapes." Matt started up the stairs, and then paused as he looked back at Davis. "What's the matter?"

"There... aren't any," Davis whispered.

Matt looked at me and shook his head. "Let's inspect the second floor."

I watched them go upstairs. Davis was talking a blue streak now, telling Matt what a fine, sound building it was.

I blew smoke rings and waited.

They came downstairs in a few minutes. Davis' face was gray. Matt was writing things down in a notebook.

"Seen enough?" I asked.

Matt nodded sadly. "Nothing personal, Mr. Davis, but the city's making a public-safety drive and..."

His shrug was pure eloquence.

"Sorry, Mr. Davis," I said. We started for the door.

"Wait." A pale ghost of a voice. We turned. "Please," he said, "if you..."

"The city always plays square with public-spirited citizens, Mr. Davis. You know that." I whipped out the quitclaim and inked in the figures. "Sign here."

"But this says a thousand!" He was strangling. "You said—"

"Property goes up, it comes down. You're a public-spirited citizen, Mr. Davis!"

He almost died. But he signed.

Driving back to City Hall, Matt was bleak and withdrawn. It worried me. We had pulled some pretty rough ones in the last two months but the Davis deal was one of the rawest. I was trying to jolly him out of it when we passed the Center Hotel and I saw Pete Lombard walking down the steps, carrying his inevitable briefcase.

Inside that hotel was silken sin. And money. A steady stream of money from the mill hands, the oil boomers.

"You know how much that fat slob collects each week?" I snarled. "Ten thousand, easy. Six cathouses, a dozen poker joints going full blast, night and day." I was choking with rage. "I created a new con for these crumbs. We've made them a cool fifty grand in leases so far, and what do we get? A lousy five hundred a month—with promised bonuses."

"You're getting a bonus tonight," Matt said quietly.

"Huh?" My rage evaporated. "Why didn't you tell me?"

"It's a conditional bonus." He smiled faintly as I pulled into the City Hall parking lot. "Come on upstairs and I'll tell you about it."

The office was a twenty-by-thirty glass and chrome layout on the second floor. Our two secretaries became very busy as we walked in. I told one of them to trace title on Mr. Davis' two acres, than walked further back to our private office.

Matt was already on the phone. "Yes sir. Tonight, Mr. Murdoch, I'll tell him." He hung up. "You're to finish sewing up the Larkspur Street options today. He wants them tonight."

"But there's no oil—"

"The City Planning Commission authorized the new civic center site this morning," he said patiently. "You want I should draw you a picture?"

I whistled softly. "A thousand feet of frontage, including two intersection corners!"

"He mentioned a fat bonus. And you'll be promoted to helping Lombard with the collections."

"That's bad!"

Matt shrugged, and that shrug should have been an alarm bell, but I was on fire with the idea that I was finally being taken into the fold. For two months I'd followed orders, kept my mouth shut, taken their crap, and made money for them. They thought they were big-time operators with their bookie rakeoffs, their pitiful garbage-hauling contract payoffs, their slot-machine graft. They'd never even heard of the numbers racket, had no idea of the thousand-a-day take a dozen good gage pushers could bring. They lived small and they thought small. Once in the fold, I'd show them! My mouth watered thinking about it.

I got out the Larkspur file and stopped dead. Matt was cleaning out his desk.

"What the hell?" I stood staring at him.

"I forgot to tell you," he said blandly, "I asked for a transfer this week. To the City Auditor's Department. They okayed the transfer this morning."

"Are you crazy? That job only pays four bills a month!"

He went right on emptying out drawers, a stubborn set to his mouth. I watched him, trying to figure it out. Then it came in a blinding flash of clarity.

"The City Auditor's Department," I said softly. "Access to all the civic expenditures, the construction bids. Well, well. So you've had an ulterior motive all the time. Young Galahad, playing the spy. You poor chump, do you really think you can get anything on them?"

Mart's lips were pressed tightly. He made a neat stack of his belongings on the desk blotter.

"Don't get me wrong," I said. "I want to smash Murdoch, too. But for different reasons. Lots of luck, kid. You'll need it."

Matt ignored my outstretched hand. "Just stay out of my way,

Norm. As far as I'm concerned you're worse than Murdoch. You've got a greater capacity for evil. If you try to stop me, I'll kill you."

I sat looking at this stranger that had once been my brother, and I felt a warm empathy, and also sorrow. But the die had been cast thirteen rotten years ago. Neither of us would ever change.

"Good hunting," I said, and his nostrils flared. "Relax, I won't spread it around."

The door closed behind him. I sat there, feeling tired and alone.

It was a hectic afternoon. I sifted titles, made confirming phone calls, and nearly drove my stenographers crazy. At four o'clock there was only one Larkspur lot that was open. It belonged to a man named Hermann.

Old man Hermann who had given me a pin-setting job fourteen years ago, when I needed a job terribly.

At four in the afternoon the bowling alley was almost deserted. Grandma Hermann sat at the cash register, benevolently watching the two teen-agers who were bowling duck-pins. The boy was tanned and handsome, with a crew cut. The girl was laughing as she made a spare, a pretty girl with long, slim legs. I watched them with a nostalgic ache, remembering, and Mrs. Hermann said, "You want to bowl, ja?"

"Where's Mr. Hermann?"

She motioned toward the hallway, and I walked slowly past her into the back room.

He was all alone, at the snooker table concentrating on an impossible bank shot.

"Dummkopf," he said sadly, muffing it, and then he looked up, recognized me. His face burst into a wrinkled grin. "Norman! He finally comes to see the old man. I hear you are a big operator these days, Norman."

"Just small potatoes." My smile felt nailed on. "Incidentally, I've got a check in my pocket already made out to you. A check for three thousand dollars."

I went right into my spiel, but it was strained and awkward and the words tumbled out like lead. As I talked, Hermann's smile slowly congealed, the scorn in his eyes was a naked thing. Who did I think I was kidding?

"They told me," Hermann said, looking at the snooker table. "One hears stories. I did not believe them. You were a good boy once, Norman. A little wild, perhaps, but a good boy. What happened to you?"

I said desperately, "The city had planned a park—"

"Indeed? A park made of oil wells! Mein Gott, how stupid I must look. Get out."

"Now take it easy," I whispered. "Any geologist will tell you there's no oil—"

Deliberately, he turned his back on me and racked up his cue. Something snapped. I grabbed him by the shoulder. "Listen, you goddamn old idiot—"

"Please." He was coughing violently. I let go. He stumbled over to the water cooler, strangling, and popped a capsule into his mouth. His Adam's apple worked convulsively as he gulped the water.

"My heart," he said with as much dignity as he could muster. "The doctors say I must never get excited. You excite me, Norman."

"If you're holding out for—"

"Good day, Norman."

I walked slowly back to City Hall in the gathering dusk. My one big chance, and I had failed. Failed like an amateur. Now take Angelo Ventresca. He wouldn't have failed. Angelo would have found a lever, a gimmick.

But I wasn't Angelo. I was a hunger-crazed rat in a crystal cage, drooling at the food just beyond the bars. When Murdoch discovered the missing option he would smile gently and place the food a little closer, but still out of reach. Murdoch knew how to punish a man.

As I climbed the City Hall steps I passed Matt and Laurie. They were just leaving. Matt nodded to me stiffly. Laurie's smile held a touch of pity.

I went up to my office, pricking myself with failure, feeling consumed by a nagging hatred for Murdoch, and mere was a pint of Old Overholt in the lower drawer of my desk. It took me four hours to kill that pint.

At eleven o'clock I stood in the foyer of Murdoch's home taking in the quiet splendor of his living room. That room was the index to Murdoch's personality; it was meant to make you feel dwarfed and insignificant, and it did. An eight-foot-wide stone fireplace, fronted by a magnificent tigerskin rug; overhead an immense vaulted ceiling; in the corner standing sentry, a gleaming suit of armor with a spiked mace. The spiked mace would have been an anomaly in any living room but Murdoch's.

Kropke, the butler, ushered me in with his usual funereal smile.

"Clem's expecting me." I started across the acre of jade oriental carpeting.

Kropke said with icy satisfaction, "He's in the game room, sir. You may wait by the fireplace."

"Big game, I suppose?" I wanted to hit him.

"Quite. Might I fetch you a drink?"

I said yes and went over to the gray leather couch in front of the fireplace.

"Likes to keep people waiting, doesn't he?" The voice was throaty, sensual. I blinked down at her. She was half-lying on the couch in a crumpled swirl of emerald silk, white frothy ermine and golden hair.

"If it's business, walk right in." Her cat smile. "The devil's playing for souls tonight."

"He's got mine."

"So you're Norm Sands," she said softly. "Clem's new hatchet man."

"And you're Shannon Quinn."

We appraised each other.

Her body was voluptuous, breathtaking. Her face was a study in concavities. Her high cheekbones and enormous, wide-slanting eyes produced an effect unreal, almost surrealistic. Yet when she smiled, the aquiline features grew radiant. Kropke came into the room silently, with my Old Fashioned. Without looking at him, she took the drink from the tray and drank half of it slowly. Her penetrating green eyes made me feel suddenly naked.

I moistened my lips. "How about your soul?"

"You don't miss what you never had," she said remotely. "Clem tells me I'm the essence of amorality. He says I'm the female counterpart of Norman Sands."

It rocked me. Behind that lazy smile I got the impression of a cold alertness, a hunger. Mantis, I thought, male and female. I said uneasily, "Who's he playing poker with?"

"Bernard Kroll." Her voice was calm, matter-of-fact. "They've been in there for five hours. It's interesting to watch Clem find a man's weakness and break him. Sometimes he uses women, sometimes money. The end's always the same."

"Supposing Kroll wins?"

Her laughed was warm music. "You're priceless!"

"No I'm not."

It was like watching two different women. A moment ago she had been sleek and deadly as a feral thing. Now her face held a little-girl wistfulness, forlorn and defeated.

"It's a rotten game," she murmured. "Kroll's in love with me. Clem wanted to make sure." Her green gaze was vibrant, searching. "I wonder," she breathed, and she was talking to herself, not to me. Suddenly she leaned her blonde head on my shoulder and gazed into the fireplace.

I was beginning to feel that pint. I looked down at her taut silken breasts and my pulse was hammering.

Most women, like Laurie, identify sex with an acute emotional need. But there is another, rarer type of woman. The type that often die violently at the hands of a lover. These women are elemental; they use sex as a deft and terrible weapon, the way Shannon was using it now.

She stirred against me with a contented sigh, and this was madness.

I tried to tell myself that we were both a little drunk, that she was Murdoch's property and we were in his living room. It didn't matter. She wanted me to have her—here, now, on that tigerskin rug by the fireplace, and I had as much choice about it as a drowning lemming.

I kissed her. Her lips were moist and plush. Her long body moved scaldingly against mine, her breath roaring in my ears. Then she moved away, delicately. She was standing with her back to the fireplace, her eyes bright with triumph.

"Come here," I said thickly.

"You can't afford me, darling."

I lit a cigarette with trembling fingers. "You bitch," I said.

"You'll be able to afford me some day. Eventually, darling."

I heard voices in the hallway. Murdoch's metallic laughter, then Kroll's voice, an agonized, croaking thing. Shannon stood, cool and regal, her hair soft gold on her shoulders. She was watching Murdoch.

Kroll's face was shiny with sweat. His eyes were wild. "Please," he said, "we can work something out."

"Kropke," called Murdoch, "bring Mr. Kroll a drink. Something strong. Now you're being reasonable, Bernard. Of course we'll work something out. I'm going to make you a rich man, Bernard."

Kroll slumped wretchedly on the couch. Murdoch came forward smiling. His face was the color of old ivory. He had just won another soul.

"Sorry to keep you two waiting." His hard gaze softened as he looked at Shannon. Then he saw the cocktail glass lying on the rug. Nothing changed in his voice or his eyes.

"Bernard's finally joining the grafters at the public trough. Tomorrow he's accepting a juicy paving contract, right, Bernard?"

Kroll nodded dully. There would be a joker in this paving contract. A fatal, concealed joker that could destroy him any time Murdoch wished.

"The options, Norman?" Murdoch was waiting and I took them from my coat pocket and handed them over. As he riffled through them, I held my breath. After a moment he paused and looked at me. "Hermann?"

"He wouldn't go," I said. "He—"

"You poor, inept hustler." He sighed. "See this, Norman?"

He showed me a check for ten thousand dollars. It was made out to Norman Sands. "I hate to be disappointed," Murdoch said. "Don't you?"

As in a dream I watched him cross to the fireplace and toss the check into the flames.

Shannon threw back her head and laughed. It was shrill, piercing laughter with a thousand needles in it. Murdoch was saying, "Good night, Norman."

I seemed to float across the jade carpeting. And then I was at the door. Shannon's laughter followed me out.

The night was cold and I shivered as I got into my car. I gunned the motor and the tires whined as I whipped around the corner. I drove fast. It was a quarter past twelve when I jumped out of the Cad and ran up the sidewalk to Hermann's door. The place was closed. Inside, I could see Hermann limping across the alleys, turning off the lights. I pounded on the glass door, panting. I pounded again and he came up, querulous, then angry, and shaking his gray head as he turned away. The glass was rattling as I hammered on the door.

He turned, his anger growing, and opened the door.

"Lieber Gott, must I call the police?"

"Listen," I gasped, shoving my way inside. "You've got to play ball. There's no oil on your stinking half acre. It's the new civic center site—"

"Get out," he said, and I blurted, "we can make it four thousand," and he shrieked, "Get out. Are you crazy? Get out of my place!" And his eyes were round and popping, he was pushing me with his frail old hands, his face contorted. "Gott," he wheezed in a horrified, strangled voice, and he was beating at my face, foam on his lips. "My capsules," he said through the foam. "1 can't breathe—"

He lay at my feet. I stared numbly at Mrs. Hermann who was standing, almost in a stupor, by the cash register. She moved forward. "Liebchen," she said, bending over him.

She touched him and looked up at me. "You knew his heart was bad," she said without expression. Her face was gray and her voice was a part of the grayness. "You killed him."

Then she began to scream.

X

The coroner cleared his throat and said, "Please, Mrs. Hermann, did you actually see Mr. Sands kill your husband?"

I sat in front of the coroner's jury, wooden-faced, remembering Murdoch's quiet venom... "You dumb son of a bitch, what were you trying to prove!" And later... "Don't worry about it. They'll say death through accidental causes, and it'll cost like hell."

I kept remembering how I had tried to explain it to Murdoch, and his dry, knowing chuckle. How I had tried to explain it to Matt, frantically, and Matt's saying, "Sure, Norm, sure. I understand." And Matt's wretched smile as he backed away from me. It was like that over and over again, and the tired voice of the coroner in the hot afternoon.

When they finally announced death through accidental causes, Mrs. Hermann made a thin, whimpering sound. Then she came over and spat in my face.

I walked slowly toward City Hall. The biting desert wind blew in from the Flats, acrid and scorching, and the late afternoon sun was the color of blood. When I got to the hall, I found them moving desks on the second floor. A gnarled old janitor was methodically scraping my name off the frosted glass door.

"Hey, pop, this is the Municipal Landowners office. My office."

"Was," he said.

I stormed inside. Laurie was there, with two other stenographers from the Tax and License Bureau across the hall. They were gutting my files, cleaning out the office.

"What the hell gives?"

They stared at me. Laurie's voice was mocking. "Didn't they tell you? There is no more Municipal Landowners Agency."

I stood, shocked, and the other girls bustled out with arm-fuls of file folders. "Look," I whispered, "it's a mistake. If Kramer wanted us to move to bigger offices, he should have told us." That was it. I laughed, and my laughter had a harsh sound. "I told Kramer last week we were cramped for space —here, I'll help you with that drawer."

"Touch me," she said evenly, "and I'll kill you."

I chuckled. "Still sore about that night?"

"Grateful," she said somberly. "But Hermann's death was deliberate, wasn't it? Why didn't you just use a knife?"

Rage boiled up in me like lava. I started around the desk toward her, and Lombard's voice purred from the doorway, "Aren't you in the wrong building, chum?"

Lombard's smile was vicious. "The little lady told you, but you're real slow. You finally fell out of bed, and your name's off the door."

Laurie went out discreetly. Lombard and I were alone. I reached feverishly for the phone. Kramer was not in his office; he was gone for the day. I called the mayor and His Honor was out, indefinitely. I called the Clarion and Murdoch was not there.

"I'll see you around," Lombard said sweetly, showing me the leather sap. "Maybe tonight. Clem won't mind. Think about it," he said as I stumbled past him and outside.

Driving out to Murdoch's house, I kept trying to relax, to think calmly. When I got there his arbored driveway was jammed with the familiar Packards and Buicks. I climbed the flagstone steps and banged on the front door.

It opened. Kropke sneered politely. "Mr. Murdoch's in conference—" I put my hand in his face and shoved. I strode past him, across the immense living room, and jerked the library doors open.

They were there, all of them, the king rats in the civic corruption. They sat quietly around the long mahogany table, their faces still. Tom Bullock, Mayor Cliff Harkness, fat Sam Kramer, Matt, Murdoch at the head of the table, Kroll, the others.

"I'm sorry, sir," Kropke said excitedly at my elbow, "he burst right in—"

"Quite all right," Murdoch soothed. "Shut the door, please. Sit down, Norman."

I slid into the chair opposite Matt. He didn't even look at me.

I didn't get it. Everyone ignored me, all eyes riveted on that little

74

man with the white hair and the soft voice. The room was choked with tension. Murdoch was speaking.

"Any idea who wrote that letter, Martin?"

Martin Rand was the county sheriff. His hatchet face was dark with worry. "I only saw it once, Clem. When the county attorney called me in yesterday and started firing questions about local graft. That letter was plumb nasty. It gave names, rakeoffs, amounts ..."

"It could have been any one of us." Judge Miller's frightened words hung in the stillness.

"But why?" Mayor Harkness' pink cheeks were moist. "Clem, what kind of game are you playing?"

"Trying to find who wrote that letter," Murdoch said blandly. "It was so beautifully timed. Five weeks before election. An eager cub of a crusading district attorney who smells blood and is out to get some. The question is, whose blood shall we give him? There's going to be a grand jury inquest, gentlemen. Before the primary. There'll be a stench to high heaven and a great many red faces. We need a sacrificial lamb. Any volunteers?"

Silence. Murdoch gazed from face to rigid face.

"Goddammit, Clem!" Kramer exploded. "Who're you to pick a scapegoat? You're in this thing too, ten times as deep."

The sullen murmur of rebellion was swelling around the table. Angry voices. Murdoch lifted a hand and the room was still. He spoke with a terrible softness.

"Pigs at the public trough. Pigs with dirty muzzles that squeal when the ax falls. You'll find no gravy spots on my vest, Sam. But let's inspect yours—your Oregon ranch with the blooded horses, that five-bedroom home with the swimming pool—"

Kramer muttered something about shrewd investments and Murdoch's laughter was like a branding iron. "The houses and lots, Sam? Whorehouses and lots of money, you mean! I've preached caution, but you wouldn't listen, none of you. But you'll listen now, by God. Shall we review your honorable record of public service, Mister Mayor?"

"Please," Harkness said, swallowing. "Just tell us, Clem— who is it going to be?"

There was a roaring in my ears as I stared at Matt. He sat, chain-smoking, and his eyes held a tiny, triumphant flame. It flooded over me with a sharp, tingling pain—Matt's eternal preoccupation with the vice payoffs, the construction bids. My Sir Galahad-Benedict Arnold-bastard of a little brother.

I stared at him and his face was a study in stone. But his eyes said, "So you know?"

My eyes answered his. "You think one stinking letter can smash them? You're a fool."

His eyes insisted. "We've just begun. Laurie's helping me. Sewer cleaners, that's us." And, without sound or motion, he laughed.

"I'll blackmail you," I told him in silence. "I'll use this. For me."

"And so," Murdoch said thoughtfully, "we need someone dispensable to the organization. Someone like you, Bernard. I'm afraid you're elected."

A relieved sigh rippled around the room.

Kroll's eyes popped. "No you don't," he whispered. "You can't do it." He was glaring wildly around the table. "You can't make it stick. I've only been in this rotten mess for ten days. How can a man—"

"You accepted a city paving contract," Murdoch said icily, "subject to certain rigid specifications. A half-block of paving is already laid. Shall we examine the construction, Bernard? The hundred parts of sand to one part of cement?"

Kroll's face was yellow and old. "I'll tell them about the rest of you," he said brokenly. "I won't play patsy."

"Yes you will," Murdoch said. "Meeting's adjourned, gentlemen. Bernard, you and Norman stay. Incidentally, Tom, you'd best close down a few houses. Just for the time being." He frowned. "And break a few sergeants while you're at it. Clean up the force and all that sort of thing."

Bullock said briskly that he certainly would see to it, and they filed hastily out with much shuffling of feet and backward glances. The three of us sat alone.

"It's no good," Kroll whispered. "It's not fair. You can go to hell."

"I thought you were smart," Murdoch said with contempt. "An eighteen-month stretch for fifty thousand dollars. Look, he's astonished. He didn't know the organization takes care of its own. Fifty thousand dollars," he repeated, tasting the sound. Kroll shook his head wearily. "Deposited to your account before you leave." His words were honey and velvet. "And when you get out, Shannon will be waiting."

Kroll's mouth opened, tortured.

"She loves you," Murdoch went on, gently. "She'd run away with you now, but how far would you get? You're broke, Bernard. A girl like Shannon needs nice things, things money can buy. If you're smart you can give her those things. She's in the next room. Go to her, Bernard."

Kroll's eyes were glazed. He stared at the library door as it slowly opened.

Shannon stood there. Her hair was soft gold on her shoulders and her smile was as old as sin.

Kroll stood up, moving like a drunken man. The door closed behind them.

"Poor bastard," Murdoch yawned. "You shouldn't have come, Norman. They'll wonder why you weren't picked."

My mouth was dry. "Why wasn't I?"

"I have plans for you. After the election. Meanwhile you'll scrounge around in the gutter for pennies until I see fit to put you back on the payroll. You need disciplining." His blue stare was hypnotic.

77

"You're crazy!" I said. "My name isn't Kroll. I'm blowing this stinking town, right now. I've got a stake—"

"Two thousand dollars in the bank and a five-thousand-dollar car. That's a stake?"

"It's enough, you old bastard." I stood up. "So long."

He let me get to the door.

"Norman," he said tenderly.

I turned. He was toying with a deck of cards.

"Ten of my chips to one of yours, Norman. And you deal."

"You're joking!"

"No, just confident."

"And you'll let me deal?"

"Sit down."

I broke out the cards, peering suspiciously at the backs and corners. It was a fresh, clean deck. I took a deep breath. All right, you cocky old idiot. You asked for it.

"Straight draw," I said. "Joker barred."

"First," he said, amused, "give me a bill of sale for your Cad. I'll write you a check for five thousand."

I scribbled a bill of sale and tossed my car keys on the table. I bought fifty blue chips, grinning a little inside. Ten to one!

"Deal," he said.

My first hand was a pair of tens, an ace and two sixes. Murdoch passed, and I bet three blues. Murdoch carefully counted out fifty chips from his huge stack, then thirty more. "Raise you three," he said.

"Sandbagging?"

78

"You mind?"

"Raise you five more."

He called, chuckling. He drew three cards. I stood pat. "Your bet," I said tautly.

He pushed fifty blues into the pot, calmly. "You don't have it, Norman. You stood pat on two pair."

I raised him five, my face a careful mask. My insides were cold. He might have threes and my only chance was to make him run.

He called, and I laid down my two pair. I was sweating. There was over seventeen thousand dollars in the pot.

"No good," Murdoch said sadly, spreading his hand. He had three deuces. "You mustn't bluff a poor old man, Norman."

We played for six straight hours. And it was not a man I was playing, but a machine, inexorable, flawless. I waited with a sick, furious patience because I had, not one, but four aces in the hole. It had taken me five painstaking hours to thumbnail the corners imperceptibly—with an artist's skill, just enough to make the cards mine any time I wished. Eventually, he would have to take his eyes from the deck. And I waited, playing very tight, and I kept losing.

It was two o'clock in the morning. I was writing a check for my last two thousand and buying more blue chips when Shannon came in with a twisted smile.

"He got drunk," she said. "And he cried. But he'll go." She walked, unsteadily, to the sideboard and splashed Scotch into a glass. "For fifty thousand he'll go. And for me."

"Are you really going to wait for him?" My question sounded foolish, even as I asked it.

She came over and stretched out in the Morris chair at Murdoch's elbow, her green eyes infinitely wanton.

"She goes to the highest bidder," Murdoch said. "But she hates losers, Norman. Right, my dear?"

"That's right," Shannon answered listlessly.

"Deal, Norman."

I began playing with a blind, reckless fury. I drew to inside straights. I held kickers and connected. And I won the next four hands.

Murdoch's mouth was grim.

I had eight thousand dollars in front of me!

Shannon got up and crossed to the sideboard, her hips rolling like water, and for a fraction of an instant his gaze followed her. And in that instant my fingers moved with a flashing volition of their own— and the deck was ready.

I slid the deck in front of him. There was a lump in my throat. He cut, casually.

I dealt, picked up my hand. Four aces and a queen.

Murdoch passed. I gingerly bet two blues, praying. Don't let him pass, God, please. Just give him a pair. Let him catch, just this once. Make him stay.

He stayed. He drew one card. I drew one card.

I bet three blues and he hesitated while I slowly died inside.

"Raise," he said finally, "sixty of mine, six of yours."

My frown was worried, convincing. I called and raised ten more. And Murdoch raised again. My heart was pounding like a kettledrum. I pushed my entire stack of blues forward. "All of it," I said.

Murdoch's eyes closed. He had a trapped, pained look, but he was hooked, he had to call, and triumph was soaring through my veins like wine.

Shannon stood by the sideboard, smiling and voluptuous. Her green eyes were saying, "My price is high."

And my eyes said, "I'll meet it. Blue-mink and diamonds. You're going away with me. Tonight."

And her eyes answered, "Anywhere, darling. Any time."

Murdoch was shoving his chips forward in a slow agony. I was already on the road to Acapulco, Shannon warm and sleek beside me in the Cadillac. We were lying on the white sand at Acapulco and the sun was pure gold on her bare skin and her kisses were deep and full of promise. And we were having dinner on the terrace by the hotel pool and you could see the dazzling strand all the way down to the blue water, with the waves crashing silver and white lace. We were having champagne in our suite and Shannon was taking off her clothes with a lazy abandon, her eyes on mine as she pulled her gown over her head, letting it fall in a shimmering puddle around her feet—

"You're called," Murdoch said.

I looked at him stupidly.

"And raised one last hundred," he said.

"I'm tapped."

"That's a nice watch."

I was laughing as I took off the watch and dropped it in the pot, laughing as I spread my four aces and began raking in that mountain of blues, over eighty thousand dollars. Murdoch's grimace was wry as he spread his hand.

"I have a straight flush, Norman."

The three, four, five, six, seven of hearts.

I sat, numb. He gathered up the pot, put my car keys in his pocket. Someone was laughing. It was Shannon. She brought me a double shot of rye. I spilled half of it trying to get it to my lips.

"You're not bad, Norman," Murdoch said thoughtfully. "Not bad for an amateur. Incidentally, I ran an El Centro gambling house before the war." He gathered up the deck, the cards passing through his fingers like water. "Come back in six months, Norman. Good night."

Shannon showed me to the front door.

"Look," I breathed. "I've got to see you. How about tomorrow?"

"All right." Her expression was searching, intent. "But it's business, darling, not pleasure. Tomorrow afternoon, five sharp." She gave me her address. "Know something? It was my idea for him to break you. I wanted you to be hungry, sweet. I've got plans for you." Her lips formed a kiss as the door closed in my face.

For a moment I stared at the door, shaking in a sick reaction. I had given up trying to understand her, this bitch with the golden body. I was staring down the flagstone steps when I saw the black Packard parked across the street. Lombard's Packard.

He had waited a long time. A big man with a grotesque white face and a sadistic smile. I was finally broke and friendless. He was going to have fun.

I was edging around the corner of the house when Lombard saw me and got out of the car. Leisurely, he started across the street, toward me. He was swinging that leather sap in his right fist.

I jumped over Murdoch's back wall, tearing my clothes and crashing through the shrubbery. I ran like hell.

XI

Shannon lived in a Spanish stucco duplex on Olive Street.

It was almost six o'clock when I mounted the red brick steps that evening. The door swung open before I knocked.

"You're late," Shannon said coldly.

She wore a green satin negligee, cut very low. "So those wonderful things are real, after all," I said, looking.

82

"Sit down, I'll get you a drink."

The quiet richness of the apartment took my breath away. It was decorated in soft green and silver. The drapes were gray velvet. A single yellow rose flared from a ruby vase on the ivory baby grand.

Shannon noticed my admiring appraisal. "Yes, darling," she said, walking into the kitchen. "The wages of sin are high."

I stood looking after her, a queer tightness in my stomach. Then I followed her into the kitchen. She was pouring Martinis, her back to me. I put both hands on her shoulders and turned her around.

She stood passive, lips gleaming wetly, a tiny flame of mockery in her green eyes. I brought my mouth down on hers and her body came alive. Her fingers were deft lightning against my shirt; then her palms were roving and electric against my bare chest. She laughed softly into my mouth. "Business, darling, remember?"

She pushed me away. "You should have been here at five." She handed me the Martini. "Clem's coming in twenty minutes."

I gulped the Martini, hating her. Shannon leaned against the kitchen table and watched. "Norm, what do you know about me?"

"That you're a very expensive whore," I said brutally. "That you hate men. Is there anything else that's important?"

She could flinch, and that, at least, was something. Then she smiled faintly. "But you want me."

I said nothing.

"Once upon a time I was nineteen." Her voice was somber. "Nice, middle-class family, nice-girl nineteen. I was a freshman at USC when I married Rudy. He was a gambler, a hustler. In some ways you're very much like him, darling."

She finished her Martini and stared moodily at the empty glass. "We moved to Vegas." Her voice was soft with memory. "Those first wonderful months when Rudy's luck was hot. He was going to take me to Paris when he made his next big killing. Then his luck went sour. He... died."

"How?"

"None of your business. The important thing was, I didn't care after that—do you understand? For three years nothing mattered. You were right about my hating men." She shivered. "You want to know how I lived those three years?"

I didn't want to think about it. "When did you meet Murdoch?" I asked.

"Six months ago. He made it sound like a straight business proposition, me and Kroll. At first I didn't care. That was before I found out what Murdoch really was." She leaned forward, tautly. "Tell me what Lombard does."

"He makes the collections."

"From where?"

"All the places," I said slowly. "The Acey Deucey, the Golden Wheel, the bars and the cribs. Why?"

"And the basement crap games," she prodded. "Percentage?"

"Five, ten percent." What was she getting at?

"Don't forget the bookies," she continued. "He's on the move always, making the rounds. But not this week. The county attorney's here. The town's clean—for the moment. Tell me what happens when they leave."

"Let's play twenty questions," I said. "You tell me."

"All the places open up again, full blast. And Lombard makes the rounds for twenty percent, a double collection. It's Kroll's incarceration fee."

I shrugged, and she went on talking. Then my glass shattered on the linoleum floor as I stared at her in dazed horror. Because what she had in mind was insanity, death. "You're joking," I whispered.

But she was deadly serious. And she wanted such a little thing. All I had to do was hijack Lombard's big collection, seventy thousand dollars. That was all.

"You're out of your mind!" I seized her wrists. She looked away from me. "Look, baby, give me six months. They'll stick me back on the payroll. You want us both to get killed? Is that what you want?"

Her eyes focused tiredly. "A small-time grifter," she said. "I thought you were a man. Clem's coming soon. Get out of here."

I shook her. "Goddammit, listen! I'm going to take this town away from him, do you hear? But it takes time."

"While I wait," she said with searing bitterness, "while I let that scaly old bastard touch me, make love to me—"

"Shut up!"

"He's got skin like a lizard." She grimaced. "Dry and old. His touch makes my flesh crawl. He's got a whip in his bedroom, a silk whip. He used it on me again last night. Look."

She did something with her shoulders, and green satin whispered to the floor.

She was like the goddess Ashtoreth rising from the waves: the classic thighs, the proud, creamy shoulders, the splendid full breasts thrusting defiantly as she turned.

Then I saw them. The angry welts, scarlet and purple around her hips.

"Put that thing back on." My throat constricted.

"Look at me, Norm."

"You're crazy. Crazy!"

"Come here."

"Get away from me."

"In two weeks," she said huskily, "the big take." Her arms stole about my neck. "You're going to do it."

"That's murder." I was shaking. "Look, in six months—"

"Then come back in six months," she said softly. "Think of me at night, darling. Everytime I kiss him, I'll be thinking of you."

I slapped her and she fell back against the kitchen sink, eyes flaring. Her right hand scrabbled across the tile. "You son of a bitch," she said, her voice a serpent's hiss. She lunged at me, holding the butcher knife low.

I pivoted, grabbing her right wrist with my right hand as I turned outwards and spun. She flew past me and slammed up against the stove, sobbing and clawing for the knife that had fallen. I kicked it away from her.

"Get out," she said in a mangled fury. "Go root for pennies, you gutless wonder. Get out!" she screamed. "The back way."

I went out into the purple twilight. As the back door slammed, I could hear her sobbing.

I don't know how long I walked the dark streets. Somewhere else in the night, a sadist with a leather sap was looking for me. Somewhere else, a bitter-eyed man named Kroll was facing eighteen months in prison for the vibrant loveliness that was Shannon Quinn.

Somewhere else, Matt was patiently gathering evidence to write the district attorney another anonymous letter about civic corruption. I thought about Matt for a long time before I walked toward City Hall.

At ten-thirty, the second floor of me building was like a tomb. The dark rows of desks were sarcophagi, hushed and brooding. I found Matt in the Municipal Utility Records section scribbling under a desk lamp with intense concentration. At the sound of my footsteps, he froze. Then his right hand blurred. I stared at the gun.

"Who's there?" he croaked.

"Put it down, Galahad." I walked into the light, and he slowly lowered the gun.

Mart's mouth worked. "You almost died just now, Norm."

I wanted to laugh, but didn't dare. His fingers kept inching toward the gun. He had found something big; it was in his quivering smile, his shaking fingers.

"You won't find anything," I grunted with elaborate unconcern. "What kind of dummies do you think they are?" He relaxed, warily. "I need two hundred bucks," I said. "And I need a job."

"What's wrong with the rigs?" He thought about it. "Oh, I forgot, you're too good to get oil on your hands. All right, Norm, the owner of the Acey Deucey owes me a favor. Wait till I call you."

I said fine and he gave me a hundred. "This is quits," he said. "You never saw me tonight."

"Sure, whatever you say. Good hunting."

I walked out, half-expecting a bullet in the back. My own brother. It made me chuckle, thinking of him up there nights, punishing himself, grimly excavating the skeletons. The nicest part of it was, he was working for me and didn't know it. Later he would wish he had used the gun.

The next ten days were hell. I paced my apartment and waited for Matt's call. I drank a lot, and thought about Shannon. A tight, raw stillness hung over Mason Flats. The town was clean. The county attorney's boys—big, soft-spoken men —were here. They probed and found a ten-cent stud game in back of Bud Tolliver's poolroom and a Mexican madam with three girls in a tarpaper shack on Orange Street. They were satisfied. Finally they left.

Matt phoned me on the tenth day. The town was alive again. I went down to the Acey Deucey and shook hands with Frenchy LeJohn the owner, and he treated me with hostile politeness until I showed him what I could do with a deck of cards. Then he thawed and said ninety a week, instead of sixty. It didn't matter. What mattered was not thinking, being an automaton from seven at night until five in the morning. I needed to keep my nose clean. I had big plans and they didn't include playing the fool for any woman. So I was a good dealer and tried not to think about Shannon. On the fourth night she came in.

Like a queen she strode past the onyx bar and the green roulette tables. Kroll was with her. I kept dealing, blindly, as they came over to my table and sat down. "Let's make it a good night, darling," she said to Kroll. "A night to remember."

I dealt. They both lost. They kept losing and after a time Kroll went over to the bar, wearily. Shannon sat alone, opposite me. "His trial comes up next week," she murmured. "Let him win, just a little."

The cards felt moist and sticky. "It's no good," I said. "I won't do it. Stay away from me."

She said softly, "Clem told me to be very nice to him tonight."

"You slut."

"Lombard starts collections in two nights," she said.

My relief man finally came. I told Frenchy I was sick and he gave me the evening off. On the way home I bought a fifth of rye. It didn't help.

She came back the next night, alone. She played roulette and won and came over to my table after a time and played dollar chips. When the other players drifted away, she said, soft and urgently, "Tomorrow night ... the big collection. They'll start here, at the center of town. You can wait for them at Amy's Roadhouse, on the Flats. Slade stays in the car guarding the loot while Lombard goes in for the individual collections. You can take Slade first, darling."

I dealt, silently, not looking at her.

The next night she came again, with Kroll. They sat at the bar. Once I heard her laughter, high and silvery, and I shivered. She wore a red chiffon evening gown and her back and shoulders were tanned a creamy gold. Now they were passing my table. Kroll said hello to me and asked how things were. I said fine. They went to the roulette layout and for the next two hours my table was filled. Then the cards ran cold and my players drifted away, one by one. I sat alone, praying for my relief.

Shannon came over. "Deal," she said.

I dealt and she leaned forward, giving me an excellent view of her breasts.

"After Kroll's conviction, Clem's taking me to Acapulco for awhile."

"That's nice," I said, and it came out like a snarl.

"Two glorious weeks. And it could be you, sweet. It's still not too late; Lombard won't hit Amy's for an hour."

Kroll joined us. "It's late, honey. Shall we?"

"Certainly, darling." She beamed up at him as his hands rested on her shoulders possessively. His wrinkled brown hands.

My relief man finally came.

I watched Shannon and Kroll cash in their chips. My stomach was churning uncontrollably. I turned, threading my way through the crap tables, and got to the side door just in time.

It was dark outside, and still. I vomited quietly on the flagstone terrace.

XII

"But mon ami, you were off last night."

"So I got the flu. I'm sick."

We were in Frenchy's office. Now he leaned forward, nostrils twitching and round eyes narrowed. "You have been drinking."

"So?"

He spread his hands. "Mon Dieu, you know the rules. One cannot risk drunken croupiers, dealers—"

"Damn your rules! I'm fired, is that it?"

He looked miserable. "Rules are rules."

It was perfect. It had been necessary to waste precious moments at the bar, but it would have looked dangerously coincidental to quit the next day. Being fired was ideal.

And I still had thirty minutes to walk over to Orange Street, to hurry past the squalid shacks and garbage-choked alleys, past the dark rail junction and out to the main highway, toward the roadhouse.

Amy's place was an institution in Mason Flats. It stood just outside city limits and had survived brief morality purges and county reforms ever since I could remember. Amy bought new Fords for half the police force each Christmas.

I moved quietly through the parked cars in back, searching the front driveway with the terrible fear that I was too late. Then I saw it, the black Packard sedan parked arrogantly by the entrance. Slade, a plainclothesman on the vice squad, sat at the wheel, chain-smoking. On the front seat next to him was a briefcase containing almost seventy thousand dollars.

I found a rubbish barrel filled with empty whisky bottles. I grabbed one and ran around to the front driveway, then weaved toward the Packard with my head down, muttering in guttural Spanish.

"No tengo dinero por las muchachas. Es muy triste."

Slade sniggered. "That's real tough, Pedro. Why don't you ask her for credit?"

Drunkenly, I staggered sideways, off balance, weaving in closer to the car.

"Scram, Pedro." Slade's voice was like a curt whiplash. "Go home and sleep it off."

"Quiere beber?" I giggled, thrusting the bottle at him. I held the bottle tightly.

"Beat it," he said; then his face paled in startled recognition. His right hand darted to his shoulder holster as I hit him just behind the ear. He sagged against the horn and the sound blared through the night. I was swearing prayerful little obscenities as I got him off that horn and down on the floor and eased myself behind the wheel. I was groping for his shoulder holster when Lombard's footsteps sounded on the graveled walk.

90

I slouched behind the wheel. Slade's hat tipped over my eyes. Icy perspiration crawled down my spine. The footsteps came closer, paused; then the back door opened and the rear seat creaked heavily.

"Wake up, stupid," Lombard wheezed. "Let's roll."

I drove down the driveway to the main road, my brain spinning like a broken flywheel. If only he'd waited another ten seconds! I wondered how long it would take to reach down and grab Slade's gun.

"She damn near died," Lombard said happily, "but she came through. They'll kiss us tonight, baby. Guess how much the take was!"

I grunted, and nothing changed in Lombard's voice; he kept on chatting away. Unaccountably, though, my hair began to bristle. I stole a glance in the rearview mirror. There was a dark blur of movement.

My reflexes saved me. The blow glanced off the left side of my head and the universe filled with colored fire.

The blows rained on my head and shoulders like hail as I ducked down in the seat and jammed the accelerator to the floor. We were doing sixty, seventy, and cold metal jammed into the back of my neck and Lombard shouted, "Slow down!"

"Go to hell!"

Stalemate.

We roared through the night at eighty miles an hour as the wind screamed past the windows and Lombard was swearing, "You son of a bitch, you dumb idiot bastard." He tried to shove the gun through my spine. "I'll count five. So help me, I'll count five and that's it. One, two, three..."

He meant it. He was crazed beyond fear. He would blow my head off and take his chances. We were still on the main highway parallel to town, and the derrick jungle was thinning.

"Four," Lombard said, and I slammed on the brakes, skidding all over the highway. I yanked the wheel hard to the left as we spun and the Packard screamed like a frightened horse.

We jumped the road.

I slammed across the seat against the right door. There was the tearing of metal and smashing of glass as I clawed at the handle, and then abruptly, the door pitched open and I was hurtling through cold night air and the world snuffed out in glass and darkness.

I lay on my back looking at stars. They were thin and peaceful and a tattered fragment of moon gave enough light to see the Packard ten yards away, silent.

I tried to move, on one knee. Agony thundered along my right side. At least one rib was broken and I could not see out of my right eye. I touched my face and my fingers came away wet and sticky.

I crawled toward the Packard, my breath a dry sob. Lombard was in the back seat. Waiting for his target to come to him.

Something moved. The right rear door creaked and opened. Something flopped heavily to the ground. There was a groan. I got to my feet and floundered forward, pain like a hot knife in my side, toward the limp bulk on the ground—a wheezing thing that stared up at me through a mask of blood, cursing through broken teeth.

I kicked Lombard as hard as I could. He kept cursing in a dull monotone as I kicked him in the head again and again. Finally the cursing stopped.

It took me ten minutes to drag him, somehow, back to the Packard. I finally got him in the back seat, pushing him like a bag of flour, and fell on top of him, retching, while bells jangled in my brain.

Lombard's briefcase was in back. I hefted it, and peered over into the front seat. Slade was still there, crumpled up on the floorboards. Then I crawled out and went around to inspect the front of the car. The grille was a shambles, as was the right fender where it had sideswiped the base of the derrick.

The derrick was an old one, deserted, and the storage tank was thick with rust. This was the south corner of the flats where a few ill-starred wildcats had been drilled six months ago, and quickly abandoned.

There was a sump in back of the rig frosted with dust and sand. A fine, big sump.

It took half an hour to adjust the idling screw on the Packard's carburetor, working in darkness and searing my fingers on the hot motor. The horrible part of it was Lombard's coming alive again, his bubbling moans from the back seat.

But I got it set at fast idle finally, got behind the wheel and kicked her over. The car lurched along the dirt road around the derrick, and I threw myself out as it kept going.

The car was like a sinking cruiser. There was one frantic moment when it hesitated, half over the brink, the hood buried in stagnant oil. That was when the rear door flew open and I saw Lombard trying to claw his way out as the Packard slid grandly over the edge.

It was a good, deep sump. But I waited, kneeling, my teeth bared like an animal's—waited with a sick, hideous certainty for Lombard to rise bubbling and wheezing out of that slime, to come and get me. But there was nothing. The wind was a soft dirge.

Five miles back to town and that briefcase weighed a ton. I shambled along the highway, pain molten in my side.

The stars were dead and cold as I reeled down Olive Street. A false dawn silvered the sky as I hammered on Shannon's door.

She wore that green satin negligee and she looked tousled with sleep, and lovely. Her face drained white with shock as I grinned at her and stepped inside. The oil-slimed briefcase dropped to the carpet and she knelt, clutching it, fumbling with the clasps.

"Norm," she said, and she was crying, laughing and crying. "My darling," she said, and it was a benediction. "You did it, lover! Was it bad, darling? Was it terribly bad? It's over now, sweet, isn't it? All over. Sit down, I'll get you a drink."

I stumbled toward the bathroom, nerves singing with fatigue, and tore off my clothes as I went. They were a mess. Blood on my coat, blood on my shirt, great rents in my trousers.

I was busy swabbing the cuts on my swollen face with iodine and cursing when Shannon came in. She handed me a tumbler half-filled with whisky, and a lighted cigarette. Then turned the shower up full and closed the bathroom door gently behind her.

The whisky was good, the hot shower was good, and a steamy lassitude crept through me like warm fog as my shrieking nerves became still. Then the cold water, the icy shock of coming alive again.

I toweled myself vigorously and combed my hair. I'd have the ribs taped tomorrow. The face in the mirror was bruised and incredibly tired, but it was my face again, not a thing from a delirium. I knotted the towel around my waist and opened the bathroom door.

The living room was dark and still. I padded along the hall and she was in the bedroom.

The empty briefcase lay on the rug.

Money was scattered on the floor, on the yellow bedspread. More money than I had ever seen. Twenties, tens, fifties, crumpled in green profusion. Shannon knelt in the center of the bed, running her hands through the bills, sifting them over her breasts, crooning softly, eyes closed.

Then she opened her eyes and smiled. "Come here," she said. Her body was alabaster and ivory. She swept one leg along the coverlet and money cascaded through the air.

"Come here," she said, and her breasts were full, amazingly sculptured, perfect. "Be neat, darling," she whispered. "Hang the towel on the doorknob. Hurry, lover. Please hurry."

I threw the towel on the floor.

I did not hurry.

XIII

Shannon's clock radio woke me at nine. "Wake up, darling. Breakfast."

She wore a filmy pink housecoat that contrasted wonderfully with her golden hair and made her look about fourteen years old. I sat drinking coffee, listening to her talk animatedly about Paris, and trying to analyze the drowning sensation that hit me every time I looked at her.

This wasn't love. Love is something warm and human, like the feeling I still had for Laurie. This was a stark compulsion, chemotropic. For her I had killed two men.

Shannon was scrambling around the rug on hands and knees, picking up money. I tried to feel contempt for her, and couldn't. I tried to feel guilt, shame. There was nothing. Slade and Lombard were two-dimensional memories, unreal.

"Norm." There was something in Shannon's voice that made me spill my coffee. "Help me find the rest of it."

We hunted for fifteen minutes. We tore the bed apart and looked inside the empty briefcase. Then, for the third time we counted it. We stared at each other with a hard, mutual suspicion.

"Eight thousand dollars," she said. "Where's the rest of it, darling?"

I shook my head helplessly. "That's it."

"You're a liar."

"Dammit, there was only the briefcase—" My mouth hung open, foolishly. Fool, fool! Not to have remembered that Slade also had a briefcase on the front seat, not to have realized that Lombard's satchel contained only the last payoff, from Amy's.

"It's still in the sump." I felt sick. "Probably fifty grand, at least."

I told her about it as she lay across the bed smoking, her green eyes half-shut. "You could go back, Norm."

"Not for a million! Even if I could find the right place."

"Eight stinking thousand," she said.

"It would go a long way in Mexico. We could live like kings—"

"For a year." She laughed without sound. "Eighteen months, maybe. Then?"

The phone on the night table rang. She picked it up listlessly. "Hello?... Yes, Bernard. Of course, honey. Tonight?... Fine." I made frantic motions, and she smiled at me wretchedly. "See you at seven, lover," she said, and then hung up.

"You goddamned tramp," I said, "we're going away, remember?"

"You're going away." She threw the money on the bed. "Take it all. You've earned it."

"Listen, we can skip to Mexico! Cuernavaca, maybe."

"I can just see us," she said dully. "Six good months. Then I go back to shaking my hips in a night club. Some cheap Mexican dive where they sit, fat and greasy, and throw pesos at you. But you'll have big deals cooking, oh, yes! Step right up, amigos, guess which shell the little pea is under! For two dollars extra you can sleep with my wife."

I grabbed her roughly, and kissed her. She was limp, uncaring. Her lips were cold. I thought about Kroll pawing her, making love to her, and I wanted to scream.

"Stop it, Norm." Her eyes were wet. "For what it's worth, I love you. But it's no good, darling, not the way we like to live."

She was right. That eight thousand might just as well have been eight cents.

For the next few weeks, until his trial was over, she would be Bernard Kroll's consigned property. After he was safely in prison, she would revert to Murdoch. He could afford her; I couldn't. I thought about these things as I got dressed. I thought about Matt.

"You'd better burn that briefcase," I said, picking up a handful of twenties. "I'll take these for expenses. Hide the rest of it. The council boys will figure Lombard and Slade got greedy."

"Try to understand, Norm."

"I've got something in mind," I said, kissing her. "I'll phone you this afternoon."

The first thing I did was go home and shave and put on a clean suit. The second thing was to go downtown to a doctor and get my ribs taped. Then I walked fast, seven blocks over to North Street, to Matt's flat.

He had found something big at City Hall, and he'd had two full weeks to work on it. By now it would be ripe and rotting. It would not be in his desk at City Hall, but in his apartment, carefully hidden. I went around to the empty alley, pried his window screen loose, and eased myself inside.

One hour later I stood scowling at the shambles—the gutted mattress, the bureau drawers lying on the floor. It had to be here. I looked again through the bookcase. I riffled through Plato, Shakespeare, the Bible. There was nothing.

Then I had an idea.

Fifteen minutes later I found Matt in the Tax Records section at City Hall. I caught his eye and he came slowly over, past the clattering typewriters and busy file clerks.

"You got a minute?"

He nodded, frowning. We walked down the hall to the lavatory. It was deserted; I looked in the booths to make sure.

"It's good-bye." I extended my hand. "I'm leaving town."

He took my hand warily. "How come?"

"I got fired last night. There's nothing left in this crummy town for me. It's just that... well, you've been damned decent and I wanted to warn you."

"Warn me?" His chin jutted forward. He reminded me of a great blond bear hearing a hunter crashing through the thicket.

"I was over at the Clarion this morning," I told him. "Murdoch didn't have a job open. But before I went in his office, I did a little keyhole listening. What kind of filth have you been into?" His jaw muscles clenched and I added hastily, "It's none of my business... but I heard Mayor Harkness and Tom Bullock talking. About you. They're scared green. Certain records are missing from the Utility Records file."

I held my breath. He had been in the utilities section that night. If I'd guessed wrong, he'd laugh in my face now and walk out.

I hadn't guessed wrong.

"What else did you hear?" Matt moistened his lips.

"When you leave this building, you'll have a plainclothesman on your tail. One of Tom Bullock's Gestapo." I shrugged. "Like I said, it's your business. So long."

Now he'd snap at the bait. He would tell me where the records were hidden, tell me to take them to the county attorney, quick. But he simply clapped me on the shoulder and said thanks, and not to take any wooden nickels, and walked out.

I swore.

Two minutes later I sauntered by Tax Records. Matt was at a corner desk. He picked up the phone and spoke guardedly, eyes darting. I waved at him as I went by outside.

He hadn't dialed. He'd asked the operator for an extension. That meant somebody in the building. It had to be Laurie.

I hurried down the steps of the building, cursing myself for not having thought of it before. I cut left down an alley, running, and the pain in my side crescendoed into agony. I slowed to a walk, sick and dizzy. Thank God she lived just five blocks away.

I got to the alley corner in time to see Laurie's little convertible come to a quick stop across the street, in front of her apartment I watched her hurry up the stairs to the second landing. I counted to ten, slowly, giving her time to unlock the door and go inside; then I trotted across the street and took those steps three at a time.

My timing was perfect. She was just coming out of her apartment when I got to the top of the landing. She saw me and froze, one hand still on the doorknob. In her other hand there was a large manila envelope.

"Going somewhere?" I asked cheerfully. Laurie's face was white. "Let's postpone that little trip to the county seat, shall we?" I pushed her inside and slammed the door.

"Get out," she said.

"Give," I ordered, balling my right fist. It never occurred to her to scream. She stared at me like a snake-hypnotized bird as she slowly backed away. For just one instant her eyes flicked to the window, and then I moved in and struck.

She crumpled, and I caught the folder before it reached the floor. I leafed through it and caught my breath. This was big. Far bigger than I had dared hope.

Laurie shuddered, slowly got to her feet, then flung herself upon me like a wildcat—scratching, clawing, raking my face with her nails. I slapped her halfway across the room.

"Sorry," I said. "But we took our chances, didn't we? We tilt at windmills and break our little lance."

I found some nylons in her bureau and tied her tightly and efficiently with them as she crucified me with her eyes.

"You're rotten," she said. "I never knew a man could be so rotten."

"You've got to work at it," I said. "Where're the copies?"

Her surprised contempt was genuine.

"Just wanted to make sure." I tied her ankles and gagged her. "If you work at it, you'll be free in six hours."

I walked out of her flat with the manila envelope, whistling.

It was two-thirty when I left the photostat shop. Five minutes later I was at the bank, renting a safe-deposit box for the originals. Ten minutes after that I was walking through the City Hall lobby. Matt gave me a frightened look as I passed by Tax Records. I winked at him.

The mayor's office was on the second floor. His secretary was frigidly polite. "Sorry, but His Honor is in conference all afternoon and—"

"They're in conference about me," I smiled, thinking about Murdoch squirming, trying to explain Lombard's disappearance to a raging bunch of councilmen. "Matter of fact they're waiting for me right now."

I walked into the mayor's private office.

The big four sat there: Murdoch, Mayor Harkness, Bullock and Kramer. They glared at me as I walked to hizzoner's desk and threw down the stack of photostats with a crash.

"Read them and weep, gentlemen."

"Throw him out," Bullock said. Kramer got up and started toward me. Murdoch merely looked irritated.

"Holy God," Harkness said. It was a prayer.

Kramer hesitated. The mayor's face was ashen. He leafed through the photostats, his lips moving, and Murdoch craned his neck to look. So did Bullock and Kramer.

They read and they looked at me, then at each other. Then they read again.

Murdoch's face was bloodless. "I underestimated you, Norman."

"Where did you get these?" Kramer whispered.

"What's wrong with everybody?" Bullock demanded. He was only

100

the chief of police; this espionage stuff was beyond him. "So there's pictures of a torn-up road, pages of figures. So?"

"So the figures are double-entry water-utilities audits," I said. "And there are obviously several thousand dollars in discrepancies. And the dates on the accounts payable sheet just happen to coincide with the dates of bank deposits made by one Sam Kramer." I coughed, delicately. "They've been holding out on you, Tom. That photo of torn paving is ground under repair right now, the current low bid for a new water main down Center Street. The specs, you'll notice, call for three-foot depth instead of eight inches. The low bid was taken by Hogarth Construction, of which Harkness happens to own—"

"Shut up!" The veins in Harkness' forehead were red streaks.

Bullock turned on Kramer like an enraged animal. "You greedy, conniving louse, it's all your fault! You got us into this! You'll step off alone!"

"I didn't!" Kramer was a terrified pig, squealing in the vise. "If you hadn't run the houses so wide open—"

"You maggots," Murdoch said wearily. "You poor, blind, greedy maggots. Bleed them white, Norman. I want to hear them howl."

"Wrong," I said. "Nobody loses a penny."

"Then what do you want?" Mayor Harkness demanded.

"Ten percent. Of everything."

"But that's all there is!" Kramer gasped. "Besides, Lombard and Slade have skipped."

I shrugged. "What about Kroll's fifty thousand?"

"We've got to raise it out of our own pockets," Bullock spat. "Damn Lombard!"

"Wait a moment." Murdoch's eyes were frosty blue marbles, searching and suspicious. "How did you know last night's collection was to go to Kroll?"

My grin felt frozen. "Guessed. Incidentally, if you've got any ideas about killing me, the originals of these photostats are in the possession of a very dear friend who lives at the county seat. Once a week I mail a registered letter. Should I fail to mail that letter, the county attorney will see these originals. Immediately."

They glared with baffled hatred, and Murdoch said sharply, "I've played poker with him and I can tell he's lying. In the first place he hasn't any friends, and in the second place it's a bluff."

I smiled at them. "It's not," I said. "But even if it was, you can't afford to call, can you?"

Bullock shook his head listlessly. "What's with this ten percent?"

"Simple. We up the total take to twenty percent. I get half, you get half."

That started it off. They beat their breasts and howled. They said the houses couldn't stand the strain. I shrugged. They pointed out that I was killing the goose that laid the golden eggs. I inquired if they would rather reduce their end of it to five percent, and they subsided, muttering. Murdoch said my greed would destroy me, and I beamed at him. I picked up the phone and dialed.

"Hello," I said, looking at Murdoch. "Shannon? It's Norm, honey... Everything's fine. Get rid of Kroll early." Murdoch's eyes were blind, shocked. "... Damn right it's a celebration! I'll explain tonight."

I hung up and clapped Murdoch on the shoulder. "Like you said, Clem, she goes to the highest bidder."

He didn't answer. They were studies in dejection, all of them. Murdoch stared at me, suddenly old and tired.

"Tom," I said, "we'd better hold my brother incommunicado for a few days. The minute he finds I stole these he'll run straight to the district attorney."

Bullock's little mustache bristled. "You mean he—"

"He's got ideals," I said. "Book him on an open charge. Tomorrow I'll see him, talk some sense into him."

Bullock grabbed the phone and growled into it. It was five o'clock, quitting time for all the public servants. Matt would be leaving City Hall any minute.

I went to the window, savoring the evening breeze, looking down at the glowing web of neon lights on Center Street. Then I saw Matt hurrying down the steps, glancing nervously at the two plainclothesmen behind him.

Matt walked fast. The plainclothesmen followed him. Matt began to run.

They caught him at the corner. I closed my eyes.

After a moment I turned around and said, "Break out the bottle, mayor. We'll have a celebration drink." There was a sour bile-taste in my mouth. "I've got plans for this town. Big plans."

XIV

That first hour was the best. That golden hour in Harkness' office—the feeling of power sweeping through me like a hot wind as I told them the way it was going to be. They were sheep—Kramer, Harkness, Bullock—sheep that listened raptly, and smiled and poured more whisky. Only Murdoch sat bleak and withdrawn, the deposed emperor.

"You boys are behind the times," I told Bullock. "Mason Flats is fifty thousand, and growing! Read the paper. There's talk in Sacramento of running the new state highway through here. Did I say three more cribs? I meant five! And it's just the beginning. Did you ever hear of the numbers racket?"

They had, vaguely. I outlined it for them—the pennies, the volume, the way every corner cigar store was a potential source of revenue. How there would be just so many brokers, and we could allocate territories, and the thing would spread like wildfire. Then I brought up the dope angle, and Harkness got up, sweating. "Hell ruin us all," he bleated. "Count me out. He's insane! I'll resign quietly."

103

I slammed him back into his chair so hard his teeth rattled. "You goddamn hick," I choked furiously. "You stupid smalltown mouse! Vice is big business. Nobody resigns. Everybody plays ball or everybody gets smeared. You all step off together."

I told them what a dozen reliable pushers could do; how there was a loss at first when you had to give it away in order to hook your joy-popper. "After you get him up to three caps a day, then soak him."

Kramer leaned forward, his dark eyes gleaming. "You can set this up, all by yourself?"

"All by myself." They sighed and relaxed. "And all you'll have to do," I added, "is spend the take."

Bullock pointed out that a large proportion of wetbacks rolled their own already, and I pointed out that tea was nothing, very little profit and too much risk. Kramer said, fascinated, "Where did you pick this stuff up?"

Something stirred in Murdoch's expression. He got up stiffly, congratulated me upon my vision, and wished us all good night.

They begged me to outline it again. I did. I told them this small-time penny ante crap was over, that Mason Flats was on the map and the melon was juicy enough for everybody. We were drinking a toast to that when the phone rang. Bullock answered.

"Hello," he said. "What?" His eyes slid away from mine. "Keep him there. I'll call you later." He hung up sheepishly. "The boys got a mite rough with your brother. They took him to the hospital with a broken collar bone."

My fine mood went to hell. I said slowly, "Keep him in a private ward, under sedation. I'll have a talk with him in the morning."

Bullock said fine. We arranged another meeting for tomorrow afternoon. I was in.

I walked the six blocks to Laurie's flat in a tired daze, trying to think of some way to keep Matt quiet without killing him.

I could frame him.

Chronologically, part of those water utilities shortages matched the time Matt had spent as assistant city auditor. The debit for this month was roughly three thousand dollars. Why not bank the equivalent sum in Matt's name and bring the ledger entry dates forward to coincide? Circumstantial, but it would be damning. I walked faster—and stopped dead in front of Laurie's apartment. The upstairs lights were on and Murdoch was slowly descending the steps.

"Rather unchivalrous to keep her trussed up all afternoon, Norman." His smile was cold venom. "We had a very interesting chat about you."

"Stop plotting," I said. "You can still play God with the city council. All I want is my share. Within a month—"

"You won't live that long, Norman. Good night."

He walked briskly down the block and I stared after him a moment before I hurried upstairs. The front door was unlocked. I opened it. Laurie looked bleakly at me from the sofa.

"What did he want, Laurie?"

"Where's Matt?" she asked.

"He's in the hospital," I said, watching her face whiten, "and he'll get killed unless you keep your mouth shut." I told her what would happen unless she played along, and she lit a cigarette with shaking fingers. But she did not cry. I admired her for that.

"What did Murdoch want?"

"Information," she said with weary contempt. "Your past background. I told him you were some sort of grifter in Los Angeles. Strictly small-time gutter stuff."

My chuckle sounded forced and weak. Murdoch was grasping at straws. Laurie gazed at her cigarette. "My fault," she said softly. "Matt got into this cesspool because of me." She looked at me, her eyes wet. "Did you know that? That I used him? Not because I wanted to clean up the town. Because I wanted to hurt you. God, the nights I've stared at the ceiling, hating you." She laughed harshly.

"Look, I'll make it up to you. If it's money—"

"Please go away," she said.

I arrived at Shannon's apartment a little after ten. She was ecstatic over the magnum of champagne and we had quite a party. But I was worried about Murdoch. And I kept remembering Laurie's stricken face and a strange jealousy toward Matt tore at me. Shannon noticed it.

"Darling, you're not very... wanton, tonight."

"I'm tired."

"Poor darling, I'm a demanding bitch. There. And there. Better?"

"Fine."

"I love you," she said.

We finally slept. My dreams were vague and horrible.

"Norm."

I sat up, bathed in cold sweat. Shannon was sitting tensely at the foot of the bed. She handed me a lighted cigarette. "You kept yelling," she breathed. "You kept yelling for a girl named Laurie."

I chuckled uneasily. "Go back to sleep."

But when I finally dozed off she was still sitting there like a sleek, jealous cat.

Next morning I went down to the hospital. Matt's room was on the second floor. The plainclothesman at the door nodded politely and let me inside.

"Hi, soldier."

Matt was propped up in bed, very pale, with one arm and shoulder in a cast. "Thought you were leaving town."

"They wanted me to talk some sense into your fat head. They want to make a deal."

"What kind of deal?" He was watching me with a strange, distant smile.

"Money," I said cautiously. "Five thousand, maybe. You and Laurie could go away, make a fresh start—"

"You fingered me, Norm, didn't you?" There was no anger in his voice, no scorn, only weariness.

"All right," I said. "But it was for your own good. Listen, if you don't play along, they'll smash you. They'll deposit money in your bank account, a deposit to match those utilities shortages. Listen—"

"No deal," he said, leaning back on the pillow and closing his eyes. "Get out, Norm."

Two hours later I walked into the bank and deposited three thousand dollars in Matt's account. I kept telling myself it was strictly a precaution, that Matt would change his mind. But I knew he wouldn't. Then I thought about Shannon and felt a little better.

That afternoon I met with Kramer and Bullock at City Hall. They had thought things over. They were worried, skeptical that I could deliver.

I pounded on the desk and said they were frightened old women, that I'd handle the delivery end in my own way. "And don't worry about Matt," I told Kramer, showing him the deposit slip in Matt's name. "We've got a mortal lock on him."

Kramer looked at me with respect. "Very sharp. When are you going after the first batch of... ah... merchandise?"

"You mean Heroin?" I enjoyed watching him flinch. "Tonight." Then I asked how Murdoch was taking it.

"He left town last night." Bullock was nervous. "Any idea why?"

I had, but it was ridiculous. Still, it wouldn't hurt to have an ally. When Kramer went back to his own office, I said to Bullock, "I've got a feeling Harkness is going to resign soon. He's weak, afraid. Have you thought about the mayoralty, Tom?"

"You know Clem," he said, trying to conceal his longing. "He thinks I'm just a cop. Kramer's next in line."

"Maybe not," I said, watching the idea sink into him and take hold. "Clem can be handled. You and I could make a pretty good thing of this town, Tom. Think about it."

He would lie awake nights thinking about it, I knew. And without realizing it, he would be a little more respectful toward me, unconsciously associate me with survival. That was important. I told him not to worry about Murdoch and to phone me at the Caesar Hotel in Tijuana if anything happened in the next few days.

Later in the afternoon I bought a Lincoln convertible. It was black and low, with beautiful snow-white trim. It was a surprise for Shannon. I phoned her and said, "Pack your things, angel. Tell that damned Kroll you're going upstate for a week to visit a sick aunt. We're going south of the border."

Those first three days in Tijuana. The sleepy-faced street peddlers following us like harpies. Everywhere the seething undercurrent of greed, the brown hands clutching for the tourista, for his Yankee dollars. Shannon, drunk in our hotel suite at dawn, alone and weeping. Weeping because I prowled the midnight streets, the flyblown bars, alone. I was looking for a man called El Gordito. Angelo Ventresca had once told me about El Gordito. "Anything for a price," Angelo had said. "Women, horse, anything."

It was like that for three days—the hundred tiny bribes, the impassive brown faces, the negative shake of heads. I felt baffled, furious. I was handling this like some punk amateur. Ultimately, I would ask the wrong bartender and wind up in some fetid Mexican jail.

We tried Caliente on the fourth day. Shannon loved Caliente with its dog races and cockfights and horse races at which you always lost. She would swear and tear up her tickets as the horses passed the home stretch in golden thunder. We lost a thousand dollars in two days. We drank too much, made too much love in the tropical nights. I discovered a wild insecurity in Shannon. She was stiflingly possessive. She had a habit of kissing me awake at dawn and asking me if I really loved her. She dulled the edges of my perception, almost making me forget why I had come to Mexico.

Then on the sixth day, I found Rita.

We were at a Rosarita Beach hotel. Shannon drowsed next to me on the salt-white sand, glistening with sun-tan oil. "You're like a caged leopard," she complained. "Lie down, and tell Shannon about Paris."

This Paris thing was an obsession with her. I knotted my white terrycloth robe with savage jerks, wanting to stuff sand into her mouth.

"I'm going into the bar. I've got to think."

I walked past the coca palms by the pool, past the bronzed, laughing volleyball players, and into the hotel bar. Big dealer Sands! I thought about the wild promises I'd made to Kramer and Bullock, and I wanted to vomit. If I came back to town empty-handed, they would investigate, find out about the safe-deposit box, learn that I had bluffed about having a friend in the county attorney's office. When that happened, they would stamp me out like an annoying cockroach. I sat at the bar and shivered. Then I looked up and saw her.

She sat alone by the terrace window overlooking the ocean, fondling her Daiquiri. Her body was ripe and full, the arrogant badge of her profession. Her eyes were hot and black, roving. They met mine. She smiled, moistened her lips nervously.

She was obviously a hustler, but that part of it didn't matter. What mattered was that long-sleeved cocktail dress she was wearing in this heat, and the tiny pin-point pupils of her eyes.

I went over to her table, trying to grin. "Waiting for somebody?"

"Not now." A slow professional smile.

She was high all right, but not on liquor. She had it, the big habit. It was in her too shrill laughter, and in those eyes with the contracted pupils, eyes that had dark circles under them.

"The name is Rita," she said softly.

Her room was on the second floor. She shut the door, smiling vacantly, and swayed toward me. "Honey, you won't mind giving me my present now? It's just that—"

I laid a twenty-dollar bill on the dresser. "Take it off," I said. "Just the dress."

Her smile faltered. "Just the dress, honey?"

I grabbed her by the wrist and flung her, sprawling, on the bed. I held her like that, my fingers clenched in her hair, and her eyes were wild with fear.

"You didn't say it was going to be like that," she whispered. "The house dick's my friend—goddammit you're tearing my sleeve—"

I slowly brought her bare left arm around. We both stared at the blotchy forearm, at the tiny red kisses of the hypodermic.

"Where did you get it?" I asked her.

"None of your damned business!" She tried to bite me. I held her spread-eagled on the bed, grinning down into her panicky face.

"Don't say vitamins or cold shots or morphine," I said. "Not with that arm, baby. Or those eyes. You had a lift not one hour ago. How many caps you shooting a day—five, six? Look, I just want to make a buy. A big buy."

A choking spasm went through her. All at once she went limp. "Is that all? Just a buy? You're not a Fed?"

"This is Mexico," I reminded her, getting up. I went over to the dresser and placed another twenty on top of the first one. "Well?"

"Why didn't you just ask me?" she said sullenly, massaging her wrist. "I hate rough stuff."

"You were high. You would have laughed in my face. It takes shock. Two to one you need another fix, right now."

Her nod was very tired.

After a time, she began talking.

110

XV

When I left Rita's room I was whistling. I went downstairs. Shannon was no longer on the beach. I looked around the pool and in the bar, and finally stopped whistling. I went upstairs to our suite.

She was still in her white satin bikini, sitting cross-legged on the bed. As I came in and closed the door, she gave me a bright twisted smile.

"You weren't gone long," she said. "How was she, darling?"

At first glance she didn't look drunk. Then I saw the empty pint on the rug, the pint that had been full this morning. There were tearstains on her cheeks, and then her right hand slid beneath the pillow and came up holding a tiny automatic.

"I saw you go upstairs with that slut." Shannon's voice was flat, utterly drained of emotion. "You lied to me, darling."

I couldn't speak. The gun was a pitiful toy, a .22 caliber pearl-handled boudoir special, but at five feet quite capable of perforating my skull. This was crazy!

"Jealousy's all right in its place," I tried to smile, feeling my lips twitch, "but this was business. I never touched her."

"Get into the bathroom." She got off the bed, swaying on her feet.

I started around the bed, trying to explain, talking very fast, and she said, "In the bathroom. Hurry."

The gun prodded my spine. I wheeled. My right elbow caught her flush on the temple.

For just one agonizing moment she teetered blindly backwards, the gun swinging up at my face; then she slumped to the rug. I was breathing hard as I recovered the gun. I wanted to break her neck, but mingled with my rage was a queer, excited pride that she could be so jealous over me. I picked her up gently and laid her on the bed. Her eyelids fluttered, opened. She turned her head away and burst into tears.

I let her cry it out on my shoulder. She cried for ten full minutes. After a time she said in a small, tortured voice, "It was four years ago, in Vegas. Rudy and I had been married a few months. I loved him terribly. He had Irish-blue eyes and a sad smile and the gentle white hands of a gambler. He used to talk about making his big killing, how we'd go to Paris ..."

Her voice broke and she turned her head away. Then she went on, rapidly.

"Sol owned half the club. Fat Solly with his golden smile and the way he had of looking at you that made you want to take a bath. Rudy played with Sol, day and night. Sol kept beating him, rubbing it in. Then Rudy got a theory about gambling, something about the psychological factors involved in winning, about guilt complexes— how Sol wanted me, but was basically a very moral man. Rudy figured it all out and finally laid it on the line. He wanted me to sleep with Sol—"

"Stop it!"

"I would have died for him," she said simply. "The theory worked. Rudy won thirty thousand from Sol that next night, playing head-to-head stud. He told me I was wonderful, that he loved me." She shivered. "Only he didn't touch me for a week after that. It scared me. Then he ran off with a cigarette girl named Lorraine."

"Look, I don't want to hear about it."

"He came back in three months. Sad-eyed and smiling and broke. Lorraine had picked him clean. He said he still loved me, that we could pick up again where we left off. We got drunk that night. Rudy kept talking about Paris. I was crying when I drove the car into the motel garage and left the motor idling, with him in the front seat, out cold. Carbon monoxide," she breathed in a dry, terrible whisper. "I killed him." She began to laugh, almost hysterically.

Then I started talking quietly, telling her how much I loved her. After a time the haunted, mad look went out of her eyes. She nestled close to me with a little sigh and I stroked her the way you would a frightened kitten.

"I'll steal for you," she said breathlessly. "I'll kill for you, anything— provided there's no other woman, ever. You think I'm crazy?"

"No," I said, holding her close, tenderly. "You're not crazy."

We sat like that for a very long time. Finally Shannon squeezed my hand and said, "Tell me about Paris, darling."

That afternoon we checked in at the Caesar, in Tijuana. After dinner we went down to the Casa Del Luz. The Casa was on the west end of Tijuana, strictly for the touristas. We sat near the dance floor, drinking Old Fashioneds. I looked around.

"A smooth Indian face," Rita had said. "A midnight-blue suit and pomaded hair."

He sat in a shadowed corner booth, a handsome copper-faced Mexican. Occasionally someone would pause at his table and there would be a brief, furtive exchange.

Casually, I got up and strolled over to his table. "Buenos dias." I accented it nasally. "Business good?"

Those dark liquid eyes raked me. "I do not believe I have had the pleasure, senor."

"But you know a man called Morales. You can direct me."

His smile was infinitesimal, a mere twitch of his upper lip. I reached into my pocket and dropped a twenty on the table. He looked bored. I added two more twenties and the boredom vanished.

"You have, of course, references?"

"I'm a friend of Rita's. I want to make a buy." He didn't even blink. "If it helps, I'm also a friend of Angelo Ventresca's."

He smiled then. His brown grasping fingers moved and the money vanished. He scribbled something on a card and handed it to me. "Take this to the Jai-Alai Palace. The runner in the chartreuse beret."

At the Jai-Alai Palace Shannon and I watched the runners in their colored berets scurrying down the aisles, taking bets as they quoted the changing odds in a metallic chant. The one with the chartreuse

113

beret bobbed past the seats, hesitating, then turning in my direction as I raised my hand.

"Quiere?"

He was frigidly polite. I handed him the card and he squinted at it. He gave me a flashing smile. "You are a friend of Senor Ventresca's?"

I nodded and he tossed his beret to another runner, smoothing back his oily blue-black hair. "Andale," he said happily, staring down the aisle.

"See you at the hotel," I told Shannon, kissing her. "Don't wait up."

I followed my guide past the bar to the rear of the building, and outside. We walked down a dark, cobbled alley and stopped about fifty yards from the street. It was very dark and still. My guide turned, a tall indistinct figure.

Steel glimmered. He came at me.

He moved with the gliding crouch of a ballet dancer, holding the blade down low, and I stepped backwards until the cold, wet wall of the building slammed into my back.

"Hold on," I gasped. "I only wanted—"

"El Gordito is dead. You wished to see him? Bien!'"

I stumbled sideways as he came in, grabbing at his wrist as I fell. For a moment his hand came free and pain slashed in a scarlet blaze across my ribs. We wrestled in frantic silence for that knife. He was strong, with a writhing steel strength that battered my head against the cobblestones again and again. My grip on his wrist was slipping. Suddenly I let go.

He fell sideways, off balance, and I slugged him. As he slumped, I brought my palm in a sweeping arc against his throat. He gagged and collapsed.

I got to my feet, fighting nausea. He lay face-down in the alley, retching. I picked up the knife and panted, "What the hell's the matter with you?"

"Kill me," he said dully, "get it over with."

"Explain, you hijo de una perra."

"El Gordito was my friend." He rubbed his throat. "Senor Ventresca killed him, nine months ago. An argument over prices, deliveries."

I began talking quickly with a rage that was as convincing as it was real, and he finally breathed, "You are an enemy of Ventresca's? You come only for merchandise?"

"Brilliant," I snapped. "So who do I deal with now?"

"I know a dealer. One Senor Morales. But there is a price." He peered at me.

"I've got it," I said.

We went to see Senor Morales.

It was dawn when I got back to the Caesar. I was tired and aching, but there were two full pounds of Grade A merchandise in the trunk of the Lincoln. Senor Morales had come through.

We were having breakfast in bed that afternoon when the bellboy brought the telegram to our suite. It was a telegram from Tom Bullock.

It took me five minutes to digest that telegram. Five long minutes, feeling the dull sickness of defeat, wanting to scream. Shannon saw the expression on my face. "Darling, what is it?"

"Murdoch," I said, crumpling the telegram. "He's back in town. He brought some strangers with him. Pack your bags."

It was seventy miles from Tijuana to Mason Flats. I made it in exactly fifty-nine minutes. There was one bad moment at the border when the guard asked what we were bringing back, but Shannon laughed and showed him the cheap silver bracelet and I said we were honeymooners, and he winked lewdly and waved us on. They never stopped you on a Sunday afternoon.

All the way back I drove in a quiet madness, hating Murdoch and praying that Bullock had been mistaken.

When we finally hit Mason Flats, I drove down Center Street and parked in front of the Golden Wheel Hotel. I told Shannon to call Bullock immediately and tell him where I was. Then I walked through the lobby and around back to the game room.

Bullock hadn't been mistaken.

Three men sat in a corner booth drinking. One was smoking a cigar and talking quietly, his gorilla shoulders hunched forward. He looked up and saw me. He stopped talking.

I walked past the roulette tables, my eyes steady on his vulpine face. Around his eyes and across the bridge of his nose there were faint purplish pockmarks—scars I had given him from burning matches almost a year ago.

"Hello, Angelo," I said.

XVI

"Well, well," Angelo said. "Long time no see."

"You look prosperous," I remarked.

"You got to keep up a front." He smiled. "Sit down."

I looked at this soft-spoken Neanderthal and at his two storm troopers. They sat enjoying it, waiting for the farce to end. Waiting for the signal that preceded execution.

I pulled over a chair from an empty table and sat carefully, watching everyone's hands. "How's Paul?"

"Ingrahm?" His old sorrowful grimace. "He had an accident six

116

months ago. Very sad. Fell off his yacht near Catalina. Drunk and couldn't swim. It was just as well; the grand jury was reaching for him."

"And he sort of willed things to you," I said.

"Sort of."

"So what brings you to this tank town?"

"Santa Claus," he answered. "A little Santa Claus that drives a Buick instead of a sleigh. A Santa that comes along when business is very slow—in fact, because of grand jury investigations and police shake-ups, there is no business at all. And this little old Santa Claus tells us about a boom town, full of cribs and crap layouts. A town that's wide open, where all the cops live in glass houses." His fingers strayed to the bridge of his nose, caressing those tiny purple scars. He smiled with his lower lip. "A town where you can meet old pals."

"Look," I said, fighting to keep my voice level. "Murdoch's using you. The old squeeze play. We can make a deal. I'm setting up numbers territories next week, bringing in more girls. You need me." My voice sounded shrill. "I know where all the skeletons are buried. If anything happens to me, this town gets turned upside down—"

"Murdoch says we deal strictly with him. Besides, you don't deal with corpses."

His two henchmen slid out of the booth. They were well trained.

"Let's go for a nice moonlight drive," Angelo said. "We'll talk about it."

"You're a fool!"

"Let's go," he said.

We walked slowly toward the lobby, his two troopers flanking me, keeping perfect step. We walked past the crowded crap tables, and no one noticed, nobody turned to stare. We went through the red velvet drapes into the lobby.

Tom Bullock stood at the lobby entrance. He was flanked by three big competent-looking plainclothesmen. I almost shouted with relief.

"Going somewhere?" Bullock asked cheerfully. He winked at me, smugly.

"Gentlemen," I said. "Meet the chief of police."

Nobody moved. Bullock took efficient charge. "Book them," he directed. "Vagrancy, concealed weapons." He jerked a thumb at Angelo. "What about him?"

"He's merely an innocent bystander," I grinned. "Thanks, Tom. See you in the morning."

Angelo watched his boys being herded into the prowl car outside. A look of grudging respect came into his eyes.

"Let's go upstairs," I suggested, "and finish that little talk."

Angelo's suite was a plushy expanse of gray frieze, frosted glass, and indirect lighting. He poured himself a drink, and offered me one.

"No thanks," I declined. "Tell me why I didn't have you sent with your boys."

His grin was tight and cold. "You wanted to impress me. This way you hope we'll make a deal."

"We'll deal."

"Maybe. You got something Murdoch didn't tell us about. You got the chief of police."

"And the mayor," I said. "And half the city council."

It jolted him. He thought about it, darkly. "Okay, so you got the connections. What have I got?"

"The muscle, the technical know-how to set up this town on a paying basis."

Angelo was suddenly clinical, all business as he got out pencil and paper. "What's the present weekly take?"

"About fifteen grand. That includes ten percent from the girls, the crap games, the bookies."

Angelo scribbled. "You push much horse here?"

"Just started. I've got two pounds, ready to cut."

Angelo was delighted. He pointed out his connections with the eastern syndicate, and I said fine. He said a ten percent rakeoff was charity and it should be at least forty percent. I said swell. He said finally, "One organization, is that the idea? No competition."

"Partners," I said. "You and me."

He stuck out his great hairy paw and I shook it. "Bygones be bygones," he said.

His smile was as phony as a three-dollar bill. He'd play along, sure. He'd learn all the angles, who to grease and how much, and in two or three months he would no longer need me. Then I would quietly drop out of sight. I would go for a midnight swim in the Pacific with concrete water wings.

We were smiling at each other when the door opened. A girl came into the suite, loaded down with parcels. She had richly sullen lips and shimmering blue-black hair. She said, "Honey, help me with—"

She saw me and dropped one of the parcels. "Hi, Robin," I said.

"Do much shopping, baby?" Angelo helped her solicitously with the parcels. "Norm, meet my wife. Honey, Norm's me new partner."

"Charmed." I gave her my most disarming leer. "But we've met, remember?"

A dull flush started at Robin's throat, worked slowly up to the roots of her hair. Abruptly, she turned and followed Angelo into the bedroom. The door closed. There were low voices, angry voices, and after a time Angelo came out of the bedroom frowning. "She's upset," he said. "Been on a shopping spree all day. New town. Poor kid doesn't know a soul."

"So you inherited her too," I said.

"Is that some kind of crack?"

"Forget it. Look, one thing we keep straight. You'll be in on the gambling, the dope, the girls. But don't get any ideas about liquor licenses, building permits, or county graft. That's handled upstairs."

"You're the boss." Angelo was humble. He said it would be a very smooth-running organization ... no friction... his boys were no cheap punks; they were strictly big-time.

After a while Robin came out of the bedroom and nervously mixed us fresh highballs. I sipped mine, tasting for cyanide, noting the soft reverence in Angelo's eyes as he looked at her. He really loved her. To him she was a symbol of richness and wonder. She had belonged to Ingrahm; therefore she was class. And I had slept with that woman, defiled her. I revised my three-month life expectancy to one month.

We finally said goodnight and I promised to have his boys released in the morning.

An hour later I sat in Shannon's apartment drinking coffee and explaining the new set-up. "You're a fool," she said tiredly. "They'll kill you."

"Not for awhile."

"Please." Her green eyes were brimming. "Let's run, now. We can be in Ensenada by morning. We've got two thousand left. It's a start."

I smiled, slowly shaking my head.

"Don't mock me, Norm. Please."

I spoke very patiently, as if to a child. "Next week," I said, "my end will be at least eight thousand. The following week almost double that. Rule out the numbers take and the dope end—it takes time to build up a trade. But the girls will kick in fifty percent, the bookies twenty-five. Sure they'll scream, and a lot of tramps will leave town. So Angelo's importing a string of girls in the morning. Right after election," I said, kissing her, "we liquidate Angelo. He does all the spadework; I cash in. It's perfect!"

She was tearfully unconvinced. I reassured her.

The telephone rang an hour after we went to bed. Shannon answered it sleepily. "Hello... Yes, darling. I just got back this evening." Her voice turned wary. "Of course I love you. See you tomorrow, love."

"Kroll," she said, hanging up. "He's out on bail. Next week he gets sentenced." She looked forlorn. "I feel sorry for him."

"Be nice to him," I said. "Just for a week. He could upset the whole applecart."

We both lay awake, thinking about it.

The next two days were hectic. Angelo and his boys moved in a deadly pattern. They set up territories and introduced themselves to sundry bookies and madams who complained bitterly about the increased payoffs. Certain cigar and liquor store merchants could not appreciate the honor of being numbers brokers. They took convincing. Some of them took broken heads.

Tom Bullock was afraid.

"You greedy idiot," he snarled, "all day long that phone's been jangling off the hook—complaints, threats of recall petitions! The council's scared to death. We didn't bargain for an army of hoodlums, possible gang wars. I ought to clean house, throw them all behind bars ..."

"Later," I told him. "Play it cool, Tom. Wait a couple of weeks, until after the city primaries."

"Then what?"

"Then we smash Angelo behind bars. Right now he's working for us and doesn't know it."

He looked doubtful. "Just don't let him get out of line, that's all."

That afternoon I went to the hospital to see how Matt was convalescing. The tired plainclothesman was standing in front of

Matt's room, arguing with two well-dressed angry men. I recognized them immediately. John Porter and Sid Oleson, two staunch pillars of righteousness in Mason Flats. They were candidates for mayor and chief councilman on the opposing ticket.

"Any trouble?" I inquired blandly.

Porter turned on me, his jowls quivering with rage. "This is the fourth time this week we've called. The doctors inform us that Matt Sands has nothing more than superficial bruises and a broken collar bone."

"He's under sedation," I said. "You can't see him."

Porter's lip curled. "Doped so he can't talk?"

"Talk about what?"

"We think you know. We'll be back tonight. And he'd better be able to receive visitors!"

I drove out to Murdoch's house in a white-hot fury. Murdoch greeted me with distant urbanity.

"You're really quite remarkable, Norman. By all rights you should be dead by now."

"If there's one thing I hate," I said nastily, "it's a poor loser."

"But I haven't lost. Not yet."

"Like hell you haven't! You really thought you were cute, importing Angelo. Well we've made a deal, understand? We're partners."

"Temporary partners," he shrugged. "As soon as he learns the ropes, he'll kill you."

"You called Porter, didn't you? You'd tear this whole town apart just to get me. You've got a goddamned stupid obsession, and some day, sooner or later, it's going to destroy you."

He looked at me with cold disdain. "You killed Lombard, didn't you?"

"Did I?"

"You're playing out of your league, you poor little hustler. You've got perhaps a week to live, Norman. Think about it."

I thought about it the rest of that afternoon. I had to have time. Time to bleed the town white before the shimmering bubble burst. Time to think of a way to destroy Murdoch.

At five o'clock I met with Kramer and Bullock at City Hall. We arranged to have Matt transferred to Happyview, a private sanitarium on the edge of town.

"We're balancing his utilities ledger at the close of the month," Kramer said, watching me narrowly. "We'll indict him then. Depositing that three thousand to his account was clever."

"Your own brother," Bullock said. "You're a bit of a bastard, Sands."

"Us bastards got to stick together."

About six hours later I walked slowly across town from Angelo's hotel. We had spent the entire evening adding up tomorrow's collection percentages. Already the numbers game was catching on and Angelo's pushers were starting to build up a trade. The vice and gambling would become a golden torrent all knitting into an organization that needed only one strong man at the helm. Me. The vision grew, coalescing into a hard, bright pattern of power. There was only one flaw. Matt. I was worrying about Matt as that great black sedan whispered around the corner and veered toward the curb. Angelo's sedan.

I dropped to the pavement as flame thundered from the rear window. I fell rolling through waves of sounds as ricochets danced along the splintering concrete. I found the gutter and hugged it, face down.

The sedan was gone.

I got to my feet. My clothes were torn. I brushed at them mechanically. Down the block, lights were yellowing the dark windows. Doors opened. People stared from front porches.

I began to run.

"Shut up. And stop packing."

"You're not going to stay?" Shannon breathed incredulously. "Are you mad? He's hunting you, right now!"

"Quiet. Let me think."

I paced the floor of Shannon's bedroom. Oddly, there was no panic, only a cold appraisal of my chances. I had underestimated Angelo's confidence, and now I was paying.

Angelo needed me now like a hole in the head. Bullock and Kramer were sheep; they'd go along with him. And next time Angelo would not miss. Next time was tomorrow, or as soon as he found me.

But Angelo had a weak spot.

Angelo had Robin.

"Stop crying," I said impatiently. "Look, angel, I need your help. Robin and Angelo don't know you from Eve. Listen ..."

XVII

It was the waiting, the sick waiting in Shannon's apartment at dawn. By the time she returned my nerves were violin strings, taut and shrieking.

"What happened? Did you meet her?"

"She likes me," Shannon said tonelessly, pulling off her slip. "I found her at the blackjack table. Angelo makes her sit in the casino while he goes out and guts the town."

"Did he leave one of his gorillas with her?"

"Always, love." Shannon climbed into bed, yawning. "She's so pitifully bored, so lonely. I told her I was a rich widow. We're having lunch this afternoon, then a spot of shopping."

124

"Good, good. She'll be alone?"

"She's never alone. Angelo has her guarded like a rare jewel. Incidentally, she's afraid of you."

I chuckled. Shannon's gaze was greenly enigmatic. "You slept with her once, didn't you?"

"Hell no!" I said, startled. "Whatever gave you that idea?"

Her smile had frost on it. "Don't lie to me about that, ever."

"Look, honey—"

"Don't, please. I'm tired."

Shannon left the apartment at noon. I kept pacing. My throat was raw from too many cigarettes. Once the phone rang and I seized it and a man's voice quavered, "Shannon honey? Hello?"

I hung up, grinding my teeth. That damned Kroll! Why didn't he leave her alone? The phone rang again. It kept ringing. I cursed Kroll in a cracked, thin voice.

It was two o'clock in the afternoon. I drank some more coffee. Angelo was collecting today, making the rounds— brothel and clip joint—collecting the fruits of my conniving, smug in the certainty that I had fled town. He would pay Bullock off later, explaining that I was out of town on business and telling him not to worry, that everything was running smoothly.

It was three o'clock, three-fifteen. The phone rang at three-thirty.

"Impatient, darling?" Shannon said.

"Where—"

"The Parisienne Chapeau shop on East Center. They've got some lovely creations, sweet. I bought a gold cashmere beret."

"Is she with you? Is she listening?"

"Certainly, lover."

"Oh. The watchdog there?"

"That's right."

"Give me ten minutes," I said. "At exactly three-forty you walk out of that shop with her. Exactly three-forty, you got that? You know what to do?"

"Of course, darling," Shannon said, hanging up.

East Center Street. Shimmering heat waves on the deserted asphalt, all the little shops and corner taverns huddled in the hot stillness like patient old prostitutes waiting for the Friday night bedlam. I spotted the watchdog under the awning in front of the Parisienne—a tall man with an impassive brown face. He chewed gum methodically and his sleepy eyes raked me as I pulled the Lincoln over to the curb and got out. It was exactly three-forty.

I started past him, walking briskly. Then I wheeled. I threw my knee hard into his groin.

He bent double with an agonized hiss, clawing at my knees. I brought both fists down on the back of his neck and he crumpled to the sidewalk, out cold.

Someone screamed. It was Robin. She stood at the shop entrance, Shannon right behind her. I took two steps forward and grabbed her arm. She fought. Shannon helped me drag her into the Lincoln.

Across the street a man came out of the drugstore, gaping. From the rear of the hat shop came women's voices, frightened and shrill.

I was doing sixty by the time we reached the corner.

Robin was a clawing fury. Shannon kept trying to pinion her arms, but before we reached the main drag my face was bleeding from a dozen scratches. I finally pulled over to the side of the road and grabbed her wrists. "If you'll just take it easy," I said, "you won't get hurt. We're keeping you on ice until I can talk some sense into that wop husband of yours."

But I couldn't reach her. She sat rigid with terror, like a frightened animal.

"Get in back," I told Shannon. "She'll behave."

Shannon got into the back seat I drove slowly down the main highway, telling Robin cheerfully what would happen to her if she didn't cooperate. Robin sat very still, my words hitting her like stones.

Later, I realized that I'd overplayed it. Robin knew the rules of Angelo's dark world, the inexorable penalty for betrayal. All she could think of was that she had fingered me to Ingrahm a year ago, and now she was going to be forced to pay.

I slowed down as we hit the coast intersection. A green Ford shot past us and turned right at the inland cutoff ahead. Robin watched that Ford with a tight, fixed look. Suddenly she wrenched at the door handle. I reached over for her as she jumped.

For a frozen instant Robin was suspended against the afternoon sun, her yellow dress flaring against her thighs. Then she was gone.

I was out and around the Lincoln almost before the squeal of brakes had died. The Ford had stopped two hundred yards down the cutoff. A man's head poked out, staring back at us. Robin lay in a limp huddle on the concrete, her eyes closed. I carried her back to the Lincoln, swearing softly as that Ford started backing up the road toward us. "Take her," I panted to Shannon. "Hurry!"

I cut left, away from the Ford, squinting hard into the rearview mirror. I tried to shove my right foot through the floorboards, and kept it like that until the Ford became a dwindling green dot, and finally vanished.

"You scared her silly," Shannon said raggedly from the back seat. "I'd have jumped myself. Where are we going?"

"Amy's. She'll keep her there for awhile. Lucky I was going slow—"

"Oh my God."

I swiveled around, stared.

Shannon sat in one corner of the seat, her face chalky. Robin sat beside her like a great rag doll with her dark head lolling sideways at an impossible angle. She was dead.

127

"Please keep driving," Shannon whispered.

I drove, feeling the perspiration turn to ice on my forehead. "I know a place." My voice had a harsh gravel sound. "In back of an old abandoned wildcat. She'll have good company. We'll have to drive around until dark. Stop crying."

Later we watched the oil form over Robin's head.

Eight o'clock. We drove slowly along Center Street. The neons were flashing spurts of bloody light. It was Friday night—a big night for the oil tramps, the boomers with cash in their jeans, burning to throw it away on whisky or the inevitable rouged smile. As we passed the Golden Wheel, Shannon's nails dug into my wrist. We'd been spotted.

It was Shep Spinelli, one of Angelo's lieutenants. He stood in front of the hotel, his pale rodent face incredulous as he stared at the Lincoln. He turned and dashed into the lobby.

"It's too late," Shannon moaned. "We could have been in Bakersfield by now."

I parked two blocks down, near a drugstore. "Come on, angel."

She got out, smiling desperately. "You're going to phone Bullock, of course?"

We went into the drugstore. The phone booth was occupied. Shannon went into a frenzy of impatience as I made a careful purchase at the notions counter.

"Come on." I took her arm.

"But she's hanging up. Aren't you—"

"We're going to see Angelo."

"Oh, God."

She was fighting hysteria as we walked toward the hotel. "You bought a pair of cheap earrings. Why?"

I opened the box and threw the earrings in the gutter. I carefully

128

placed the box in my coat pocket. "A bluff," I said. "For Angelo's benefit. Now smile! Look brazen, honey. That's better."

Her laughter was something out of Dante.

We went through the swinging glass doors. Two big, quietly dressed men exchanged leisurely glances as we crossed the lobby. They followed us into the elevator. On the way up, nobody spoke. This was the ultimate, the most cosmic bluff of all. Fifteen minutes from now I would either have several thousand dollars in my pocket, or be a dead man. Shannon's nails dug into my palm. But her smile was fixed, bright.

I hammered on the door of Angelo's suite. It swung open.

"Hello, Angelo," I said.

The two men followed us into the suite, but they were shadows. The other men in the room were also shadows, dark nonentities beside the primal fury that rose from the sofa and stalked toward me.

I tossed a small, black pasteboard box at Angelo's feet. A soft sigh rippled around the room. "Before you kill me, open it," I said.

Angelo stopped, blindly. He stared at me across a gulf in time, and his incandescent rage slowly faded, replaced by an ancient fear.

"Where is she?" he said thickly.

"Open it."

Angelo's fingers shook as he picked up the box. He was afraid to open it. In the old days he had been a button for the Mafia. They had a lovable trick of presenting a small box to an enemy after the snatch—a box containing the finger of a loved one. Angelo's breath came in spasms as he opened the box. Then he stared at me.

"That's right." My knees felt like jelly, but my voice was cold, dispassionate. "It's empty. But unless we make a long-distance phone call in ten minutes, you get another box in the morning mail. A box with a few of her teeth in it. Or maybe an ear—"

His roar was an apelike bellow. The blow slammed into my temple and the universe exploded in a glory of crimson suns. Shannon screamed.

"You heard him," Angelo said. "You got ten minutes. Don't let him pass out."

One of them flipped me upright; another held my arms. I tried to grin. "Maybe it'll be a bonus in the morning mail, Angelo. Maybe two fingers."

A fist rammed into my mouth.

"Slop it," Angelo cried hoarsely. He reached down and grabbed me by the lapels. "You son of a bitch, is she all right? Is she?"

"At the moment," I said.

His arms dropped to his sides. "All right," he said. "Your deck, your deal."

"That was a bonehead stunt last night," I told him. "You've sure got some amateurs working for you. How much was yesterday's take?"

"Nine grand."

"Yesterday morning we estimated fourteen."

"All right," he said too quickly. "Fourteen."

"My half," I said, and he blinked. "That's all I want—my fourteen thousand. I'll pay the city council boys out of that, per our agreement. In two weeks, after the city elections, you get Robin back safe and sound. Well?"

"Just two weeks?" Angelo said heavily. His face was all animal cunning. "You say she's safe. Just to make sure, we'll keep this tramp as security. You got objections?"

Shannon looked at me with a trapped horror. "Go right ahead," I shrugged. "Incidentally, you've got four minutes. Where's the money?"

Exactly ten minutes later I was helping Shannon into the Lincoln.

"You drive." I leaned back in the front seat and closed my eyes. I had never felt so tired.

Shannon drove in a tense, angry silence. "Would you have left me there?"

"Don't be silly. If Angelo thought I gave half a damn about you, it might have been different."

Shannon drove quietly across town. My head was throbbing. My thoughts were gray as ashes. We were living on borrowed time. Angelo would watch us night and day, and it would not take him any two weeks to discover that Robin was sleeping at the bottom of a sump.

I had fourteen thousand dollars in my pocket. I had Shannon. The smart thing to do was run.

But I wasn't going to run. I still held a few high cards in this game and I was going to play them out to the finish.

We turned left on Olive Street. I caught a brief glimpse of a car parked in front of Shannon's duplex before she hissed, "Get down! It's Kroll."

I slid down in the front seat, out of sight. Shannon wheeled into the driveway and got out of the Lincoln quickly. There was the sound of her heels tapping up the walk and Kroll's car door slamming.

Kroll's voice was tired. "Where'd you get the new car?"

Shannon's laughter was high and silvery. "It's that Norm Sands. He wants to sell it to me. Says he's broke, needs money. You know Norm."

"You're pretty good friends with him, aren't you?"

"Darling, you're jealous! How sweet—"

"I've been waiting for two hours," he said brokenly. "We had a date at seven, remember?"

The sound of a kiss. And Shannon's small, tragic voice. "I'm terribly sorry, Bernard, but I thought it was tomorrow night. I've been shopping, sweet." The sound of another kiss. My insides squirmed.

I stole a glance through the vent window, and they were on the front porch. Kroll was holding her very close.

"... such a tearing headache," Shannon was saying forlornly. "Please forgive me. Not tonight."

"I get sentenced Tuesday. Four more days."

Shannon turned on the tears. She was very good. Kroll held her close, pleading. "Please, honey, marry me now. Tomorrow morning. Look, Clem's banking the fifty thousand Monday. You can live decent while I'm away."

"Let me sleep on it. Please, darling."

Kroll kissed her awkwardly. She said good night.

For almost a full minute he stood on the porch, staring at the closed door, his shoulders sagging. Then he went slowly back to his car and drove away. I counted to ten before I uncramped myself from under the dash panel and went inside.

Shannon was in the kitchen making coffee. She was drunk on the giddy reaction of relief. "Fourteen thousand dollars, and of course you'll keep the city council's share. I'll start packing."

I lighted a cigarette, wondering how to tell her. She was prattling on about Paris—how cheap it was to live in the south of France, how we'd get along. She was a firecracker of emotion, ready to go off. Abruptly I lit the fuse.

"We're staying," I said. "Kramer and Bullock get their full share. I need them."

The coffee hissed on the stove, unnoticed. Shannon shook her bright head in disbelief. Then she came over and put her hands on my shoulders.

"Listen, darling." She was fighting for control, enunciating very carefully. "If you stay in Mason Flats, you're going to die. I don't care about the damned money."

"I care about the money."

"No." Her voice was lifeless. "You just hate to lose." The simple truth.

"You're my female counterpart, remember? We like nice things. With money we're champagne's bright children, all glitter and Stardust. Without it we stink. In two years we'd be broke in some fleabag hotel, hating each other like trapped animals." I put my arms around her, nuzzling her hair. "I won't let that happen to us. I've got this town in my fist and I'm going to squeeze it dry—"

Shannon tore away from me, almost running. She threw open the bedroom door and there were sounds of drawers opening, suitcases being thrown on the bed.

I went into the bedroom. She was packing, furiously. She tore an armful of gowns off their hangers and crammed them into the trunk, not looking at me.

"Aren't you taking that black lace chemise? I liked it."

"Go away," she sobbed. "Go to Angelo and commit suicide!"

I stood watching her without saying a word, and after a while she stopped packing. She stood slumped over the suitcase like a tired old woman.

"How much money will it take?" She was listless, resigned. "How long before we pull stakes and run?"

"A couple of weeks," I said. "Maybe three. By then we'll have forty thousand. It's enough."

She took a long shuddering breath and walked past me into the living room. There was the click of the phone dial repeated four times. A pause. Then her voice, cool and husky. "Bernard, darling? I'm so glad you went straight home..."

It came over me in a white-hot spasm and I charged into the living room, shouting soundlessly, "Please, please." Her smile cut me like a sharp knife.

"Yes, darling," she was saying with that terrible smile. "I'm sure. We can be married tomorrow morning. A quick Mexico honeymoon. Of course I'm sure, dearest..."

She finally hung up, and I yelled, "You're not going through with it! I won't let you."

"Monday afternoon," she said evenly, "they deposit his fifty thousand. I can talk him into a joint bank account easily. Tuesday morning he goes up for sentence. That afternoon I withdraw it all. We can leave Tuesday night."

"No!" I was shaking. "You want to make a pimp out of me, is that what you want?"

"No choice. You can't stay, and you won't run." She came into my arms. There was an edge of cruelty, tinged with self-contempt, in her voice. "You were right about us. We both want the good things in life. The Riviera sunshine, champagne at the St. Moritz. It's the only way."

"I won't let you go through with it."

"You can't stop me."

She had a ruthless strength that I never would have suspected. I pleaded for an hour. She wouldn't listen. Finally, she looked at me with compassion and said, "I'm going to do it. Please don't talk any more."

XVIII

The Justice was a pink little man with a nervous smile.

Shannon looked like a pale death angel as he twittered through the service. Kramer, Murdoch, and I stood solemnly as if at a funeral. Afterwards, I congratulated Kroll and kissed the bride. Her cheeks were wet.

"What's wrong, honey?" Kroll was startled.

"It's just that she's so happy," Murdoch said. "Congratulations, Bernard. We'll see you Monday."

Kroll looked proud and happy as we went outside to the glittering Buick Kramer had loaned them for the honeymoon. "Why don't we drive down to Tijuana, honey?" He squeezed Shannon's hand and she shivered. "Only two days and nights, and we've got lots of honeymooning to do."

"Try the Caesar," I said, wanting to hurt her. "They've a nice bridal suite."

It brought a last anguished look from her as the Buick purred off into the noon haze.

"What a well-fed sacrificial lamb," Kramer wheezed. "I'll buy the drinks."

We sat in the dim coolness of the Acey Deucey bar. Kramer waxed eloquent over bourbon... yesterday's take had been far more than he had dreamed, he owed me a debt of gratitude for the present setup, this way there was more for everybody. Murdoch sat bloodless and glacial over his brandy. "Incidentally, Norman, what's this trouble with Angelo?"

"No trouble," I said.

"God, no," Kramer murmured. "Not two weeks before election. You promised to keep him in line."

"How about Matt?" Murdoch probed. "He's still under wraps?"

Kramer nodded with a worried frown. "But Porter and Oleson have been stirring up trouble. They've gotten quite a following in the young voter's league and the civic union. There's been talk. Yesterday Porter asked me pointblank where Matt was being kept. I had to play indignant, mad. I don't like it, any of it!"

I flicked a knowing glance at Murdoch. He smiled faintly. Kramer's eyes darted to Murdoch. "You wouldn't sell us out, would you, Clem?"

"He's too smart for that," I said.

The polite surface phrases, and underneath, the roiling crosscurrents of fear. Murdoch would have no compunction about throwing the entire city council to the wolves—if he could get me in the process. Kramer sensed this, and his smile crumbled at the edges.

I bought Murdoch another brandy, wondering how to kill him. He had something lethal in mind, I knew. Something that would happen soon. His sardonic smile reminded me of the night when he had savaged me with a straight flush.

Later that afternoon I wandered down to the Golden Wheel. I sat in the game room drinking, trying not to think about Kroll and Shannon and Matt.

I had picked the wrong place to relax. The chant of the croupiers, the rustle of cards and chips evoked too many memories. Memories of a soft, deadly voice saying, "You're out of your league, you poor little grifter." And another voice, cold with contempt. "Your own brother. You're quite a bastard. Sands,"

I drank to that.

All afternoon I bar hopped, trying to lose myself in alcohol. It was no good. Fear walked with me. Fear of a brooding Neanderthal whose wife I had killed. Fear of an icy little man whose mistress I had stolen.

By midnight I was blind drunk. Drunk enough, I figured, to go home and be able to sleep without having nightmares.

I was wrong.

Next day—Sunday—was worse. I prowled the Center Street honky-tonks, drinking, shooting craps, trying to relax. All the bartenders and the croupiers wore polite hating smiles. I smiled back, not enjoying it. I was one of the City Hall bastards responsible for the increased collections. A parasite off parasites. A big man.

I was in the Acey Deucey, trying to make a twenty-dollar pass, when I saw Angelo. He stood alone at the bar, drinking. I walked over to him. "I'll buy."

"I'm particular who I drink with." Angelo's eyes were mean, bloodshot. "How's Robin?"

"Fine."

He was very drunk. "So help me Jesus, if you've touched one hair of her head—"

"Relax, we're gentle people."

"We?"

"I told you once I owned the police force. You had to find out the hard way."

The enormity of it stunned him. "So you had help on that snatch." He knotted one hairy fist and stared at it. "Copper help."

I let him swallow the lie. "Murdoch doesn't control everything," I said. "You were getting too big for your britches; you had to be brought in line. No point in fighting it. Let's be friends."

"Just so she's all right." His gnarled grin. "Like you say, we need each other."

We smiled into each other's eyes, reading death there.

Could I stall him for two more days? By this time Tuesday Shannon and I would be driving off into the sunset with Kroll's fifty thousand. That's a nice picture, I thought. Focus on it, Sands. Forget about Robin in that sump. Forget about Matt's being framed. Poor, ox-headed, crusading Matt, playing jungle rules with a boy scout knife.

I played at that crap table for two hours, I lost six hundred dollars. Anything for some excitement, anything to forget about Matt. I finally tossed the dice on the table and walked outside.

I parked the Lincoln in front of Laurie's apartment and sat there for ten minutes, trying to figure the odds and calling myself a fool, before I finally climbed the steps and rang the bell.

Laurie opened the door. "Come in," she said. Tired voice, pale lovely face, copper hair, gray eyes cold with contempt as she stared at me.

137

I walked past her, silently, toward the telephone on the table. If I hesitated now, I wouldn't go through with it. It was a quixotic bonehead stunt, a sucker play, but I picked up the phone and dialed Bullock's home number.

When he answered I said, "Tom, I'm worried about Matt. It might be smarter to make a deal."

"He's a goddamn fanatic," snorted Bullock. "I went over to the sanitarium yesterday, tried to reason with him. The sonuvabitch spit in my face!"

"Listen to me, Tom," I told him, "you don't know how to handle him. Call Happyview right now. Tell them you're sending a visitor over tonight. I'm going to scare him into playing ball."

"Why bother, Norm? We've got him dead to rights on that three thousand utilities shortage—"

"Call Happyview," I said.

"All right," he grumbled. "But it's a waste of time."

I hung up and Laurie said quietly, "Matt won't bargain with you."

"He won't have to. You got a gun?"

"A what?"

"A rod, a heater, an iron. Matt's going to escape."

Hope flared in her eyes, then faded. "So they can kill him?"

"Listen," I said, feeling a little desperate, "if he doesn't escape, they'll either kill him or frame him. Understand? You're going to drive out to Happyview tonight. They'll admit you to Matt's isolation ward. Carry the gun in your handbag. Give it to him. He can leave it under his pillow until Tuesday night."

"Why Tuesday night?"

"I'm leaving town then. For good."

138

She gave me a long searching glance, then turned and went into the bedroom. I leaned back on the sofa and gazed around the little apartment. It was a cozy place... warm, lived in. The pink drapes, the Matisse reproductions on the wall, the walnut hi-fi that Matt had bought her for her birthday.

I could be living in this apartment now.

I could have had Laurie.

And I had traded her for a high-priced slut, an amoral, jealous wanton. No, that wasn't quite fair, I thought. In her own fashion, Shannon loved me and had her own peculiar moral code. She was proving it right now.

"Here," Laurie said, coming out of the bedroom. "It belonged to Papa. There aren't any shells for it. It's just as well."

It was a .32 automatic, slightly rusty. It would do. I hefted it. "Put it in your handbag. When you walk into Happyview tell them Tom Bullock sent you down to talk to their special patient. And remember, Matt doesn't escape until Tuesday night. You'll make him promise?"

She nodded. There was a breathless intensity about her as she followed me to the door. It was in her trembling smile, the color in her cheeks. Looking down at her, I felt the old familiar urgency ripping at my senses.

"Good night, Norm." It was a whisper.

"Good-bye, Laurie." I went out. The door closed.

Driving home, I had the feeling that I had played the fool. But when I finally went to bed, there were no more nightmares.

Monday morning I got up early and started packing. Kroll and Shannon were due back this afternoon. Kroll's time expired tonight. Tomorrow he would report to the county seat for sentencing. By noon tomorrow Shannon and I would be fleeing south.

The nice part of it was that I still held that manila envelope. That envelope meant power. In two weeks, just before the primaries, certain city officials would receive photostats in the mail. I chuckled, thinking about their frantic last-minute scurrying to raise the loot necessary to keep them out of jail.

Shortly after noon I finished packing and went out to eat. I had a steak at a downtown chop house, then drove slowly toward the bank. Now was the ideal time to withdraw that manila envelope from my safe deposit box and have a dozen photostats made of the contents.

I was being tailed.

I whipped right on Center, squinting into the rearview mirror. A tan Mercury followed. It stayed a discreet hundred yards behind, keeping smooth pace with the green lights, following me as I cut left on Orange toward the outgoing artery.

Angelo? Murdoch? The key to that safe deposit box suddenly felt warm in my pocket. I floorboarded the accelerator, and the Lincoln snarled.

Exactly five minutes later and eight miles out of town, I pulled over to the side of the highway, swearing. I got out and walked back down the road to where the Mercury waited.

"What in hell's the idea?"

He was sad-eyed and wizened, a dark little man who showed me the gun just in case I should get ideas. His name was Froggy Martin, and he was Angelo's right-hand errand boy. "Angelo says I should play cocklebur," he said gently. "He wants to keep tabs on you."

"What for? I'm not going any place."

"Angelo talks with Murdoch an hour ago. Murdoch says come Tuesday you may get itchy feet and blow away in the night like an Arab. Angelo is a very cautious man."

So Murdoch had guessed. The back of my neck felt cold.

"Yesterday I beg Angelo to let us work on you. Half an hour, I tell him, and you will be happy to tell us where Robin is. Angelo says no.

140

He says he would not like to receive Robin's finger by parcel post." He had soft, smiling brown eyes.

I was staring at the Mercury's tail pipes. "I was doing a hundred and fifteen back there. Just what have you got under that hood?"

Froggy chuckled and began expounding on the virtues of a three-quarter race cam with milled heads and duals. I walked back to the Lincoln, shaking. Froggy followed me all the way back to town.

Ten minutes before three. The bank closed at three. I began to sweat. The Mercury was almost a block behind.

I circled the block and cut right on Main, then swerved into the alley behind the bank. I opened the door and hit the ground running.

I was in the bank for perhaps five minutes. When I got back to the alley, I was carrying a certain manila folder in my coat. It felt like ten tons of nitro with a slow fuse.

And there was that damned Mercury sitting insolently in back of my Lincoln. Froggy was puffing on a cigarette.

"You sonuvabitch," I said..

"I used to be a private eye." Froggy's smile was sad, apologetic.

Whoever made up that rule about not hitting someone with a lighted cigarette in his mouth is crazy. It works fine. Froggy's head snapped one way and the cigarette another. I left him slumped over the steering wheel with the cigarette burning holes in the Mercury's upholstery.

I drove across town fast and parked on Olive, four doors up from Shannon's duplex. The maroon Buick sat in Shannon's driveway. The honeymooners were home.

For an hour I chain-smoked, watching the street for a tan Mercury.

This complicated things. The smart thing to do was run now, and join Shannon later this week in Vegas. Murdoch was goading Angelo to a killing rage. The ice was paper-thin, and cracking.

It was almost dusk before Kroll hurried out of the house and got into the Buick. After he was gone I finished my cigarette before I walked down the street to Shannon's place.

"Oh darling, darling, I thought you'd never come."

"How was he?" I said, feeling the bitterness well up inside me like acid.

"Don't be rotten, darling." She clung to me tightly, lips searching. She looked drawn and tired.

I disengaged her gently. "We got troubles. Hide this thing—under the bathtub, in the attic, but bide it good!"

She took the manila envelope without a word and went into the kitchen.

Time to run. There was still time.

Shannon came in from the kitchen, and kissed me. "In the top of the refrigerator." Her eyes danced. "In the freezer, underneath three frozen cutlets. Nobody ever looks in freezer compartments. Kiss me."

"I've got some bad news—"

"Let it wait. He'll be gone hours." She bit her lip. "Only..."

"Only what?"

"I was in the bathroom," she said slowly, "when the phone rang. It was Murdoch. When Bernard hung up, he gave me a real strange look and said he'd be gone for two hours. You don't think—"

"I think I'm getting out of here, right now."

"Hold me tightly, Norm. Darling, I'm scared."

I held her close, stroking her blonde hair, feeling the thin edge of panic, and that was when the front door opened.

Kroll stood there.

Nobody moved. Seconds stretched into tortured aeons and still nobody moved. Kroll's eyes were shocked, vacant.

"I wouldn't believe him," he said. "He told me and I wouldn't believe him. Just a fool," he said vaguely. "No fool like an old fool."

"You've got it wrong." I walked toward him, smiling desperately. "I was just wishing her a friendly—"

"Don't come near me." His Adam's apple moved. "Clem told me about you, all about you. You keep away from me." He stumbled out.

The doorway was empty. I ran out to the porch. Shannon had me by the arm; she was pleading. The Buick leapt away from the curb and down the street, the taillights winking around the corner.

"Norm, you're breaking my wrist!"

I let go. We stared at each other numbly.

"Pour me a drink," I said to her.

You plan, you scheme, you lie awake nights, and you kill. You dream of a mountain of gold, and at last the mountain becomes a shining reality. Then one slip, just one. The gold vanishes like mist in the sun. I became aware of Shannon's voice, angry and strident.

"... do something! You can't just sit slopping up liquor—"

"Let me think."

The pattern was murderously clear. First Kroll would get drunk. Crazy, killing drunk. He would slobber on Murdoch's shoulder. Murdoch would be very sympathetic. He would advise Kroll to spill his guts in court tomorrow, expose the whole rotten mess. That'd be very fine. Ten days before election. I could see Bullock and Kramer—half the city council—streaming all points west. I could see Angelo's face when Murdoch told him Bullock was no longer protecting me. Lovely.

"Get dressed," I told Shannon. "We're making a social call. You still got that gun?"

She had it. I checked the safety and slid it into my coat pocket. "Ever use this for anything besides killing flies?"

She inspected the long seams of her nylons critically. "Not yet."

"That day in Mexico. Would you have really used it?"

The sudden chill, waiting for her answer. Her flat green stare as she wriggled into her slip. She was a strange, violent woman, this Shannon.

"Of course," she said. "Where to, darling?"

We drove for a frantic hour, taking dark side streets to Kramer's house, to Bullock's. I made quick phone calls, and neither Kramer nor Bullock were at home or at their offices. I had to find them, and swiftly. We could still salvage a few thousand dollars from the ruins. Bullock would jump at the chance to get that manila envelope. And after that, there was one final thing to do before we left town. I was going to find Murdoch and kill him.

By seven o'clock I was desperate. On impulse I drove to Murdoch's house, and there was Bullock's car sitting in the driveway. I parked in back of it and got out.

"Wait here," I told Shannon, kissing her. "Be back in ten minutes."

Murdoch answered the door chimes. "Good evening, Norman." His eyes were mocking as he ushered me into the living room. "It seems we have a crisis."

Kramer and Bullock stood bleakly by the fireplace. They glared at me as we came in. It was too late for my kind of deal. They already knew.

"So you couldn't wait," I snarled at Murdoch. "You had to tell them! Tear the town apart just to get me—"

"Mart's escaped," Bullock said harshly.

"Matt?" I didn't get it. My thoughts refused to focus. I sat down, weakly.

144

"This afternoon," Bullock said. "He stuck a gun in the orderly's face, walked right out of the sanitarium. We're through. Even if we could find him, it's too late. He'll run straight to the county attorney." He splashed brandy into his glass and gulped it like water. "Your imported hoods, your goddamn bright ideas!" He started toward the door. "I'm resigning right now, taking a trip upstate."

So Matt and Laurie had crossed me. They had promised to wait until Tuesday afternoon. I moistened my lips. "Hold on, Tom. I can find Matt. I'll keep him in line."

Murdoch and Kramer looked at me, their faces white and strained. Now they were staring past me. I turned, gingerly. Shannon stood in the doorway, very pale. She moved slowly into the room. Behind her was Kroll.

"Go on," said Kroll wearily, prodding her with the gun. "Get over there, you bitch, with the rest of them."

He stood in the doorway, weaving slightly, smiling. He was blind, deadly drunk. "I knew you'd wind up here. I've been waiting. All the serpents together in their nest."

"Don't be foolish," Murdoch snapped. "I'm here, Bernard, your friend Clem. Put that thing away."

Kroll was deaf. He took four wavering steps into the room. He looked at Kramer, then at me. The gun lifted slowly, steadied.

"Cuckold," Kroll whispered. "A martyred cuckold to boot. Real funny, wasn't it?" He turned to Shannon. "How you must have laughed! Take away his money first, then his pride. Then his honor. Kroll, the patsy!" The gun came up, swiveled toward her. His finger whitened on the trigger.

My yell was lost in the racket of gunfire and Shannon's screams. Bullock knelt by the fireplace, flame roaring from his gun, as Shannon crumpled to the carpet. Kroll moved very fast, skipping backwards with a crazed grin as he traded shots with Bullock. I dove, and tackled Kroll around his knees. He was down, prostrate, as I grappled for the gun. It came away easily and I brought the barrel down to smash his skull. But he lay motionless. His eyes were blank and a red stain was creeping across his shirt.

145

Bullock's voice was ragged. "Is he ..."

"Nice shooting," I said.

Kramer was vomiting in the fireplace. Murdoch leaned against the couch, his face gray. He was smiling.

I bent over Shannon. Her hair was spread out like fine strands of gold wire, and her skin was waxen. I touched her fingers. They were cold. There was a tearing sense of loss as I explored her body, looking for the wound. She moaned, stirred.

"She only fainted," Murdoch said. His tired voice seemed to fill the room. "I've made another error in judgment, Norman. I miscalculated the extent of Bernard's passion." He coughed rackingly. "One pays for errors. Ironic that he should have missed her and gotten me."

He tottered, slumped. It was incredible, seeing the blood trickle from the corner of his mouth. It was like seeing a machine cry, a statue bleed. "Not much point in depositing Bernard's earnest money now, is there?" He chuckled. "Quite a savings, gentlemen."

His eyes blinked, opened wide. They focused on me, glazing. "You'll destroy each other, you and her. At least I'm costing you, Norman. Fifty thousand dollars," he said, and died.

XIX

"I'm getting out of here," Kramer yelled, and bolted for the door.

"Hold on!" I shoved him back against the couch.

He looked horrified. "If you're under the impression we'll be a party to—"

"Shut up," I said savagely, "and put that gun away, Tom. The whole setup's tailor-made!" I started talking fast, explaining the way it had to be.

Kramer swallowed. "He's crazy, Tom. Look at his face."

"Not so crazy," Tom said slowly. "If we can find the bullets from my gun ..."

It took us an hour to find them—peering at the walls, digging into the woodwork with penknives. Three ugly, flattened lumps of lead. I put them in my pocket, grinning at Shannon as I took out a handkerchief and picked up Kroll's gun. I carefully shot him in the chest. Shannon almost fainted again.

"For powder burns," I explained, locking Kroll's fingers about the gun. "Murder and suicide. We've got motivation, circumstance, everything. Murdoch's editorials in the Clarion exposed Kroll as a grafting contractor. He's already confessed to that in court. He came here drunk, out for revenge. He shot Murdoch, then himself. Statistics will prove the same gun killed both parties. Kramer and Bullock were innocent bystanders."

"But he was shot twice," Shannon whispered.

"Powder burns cover the same area," Bullock said, picking up the phone. "They'll find a slug from the same gun underneath him. The M.E.'ll make it open-and-shut."

He called police headquarters, lips pursed. Afterwards he said, "Actually, it's better this way. I was getting afraid of Clem. You'd better leave before the meat wagon gets here."

I took Shannon's arm and steered her toward the door. She moved like a somnambulist. "Make sure your stories jibe," I warned Kramer. "Let Bullock do all the talking."

Kramer was mush, palsied and quivering. "Whatever you say." Recollection stirred, and his mouth opened. "But Matt's still free—"

"I'll take care of Matt. See you at City Hall tomorrow, gentlemen."

"It's going to come off," Bullock said. "I can feel it." He glanced at me queerly. "I was just thinking."

"What's that?"

"You're beginning to look like Clem already."

We drove down Imperial. Shannon sat back lifelessly, eyes closed. She was spent.

"Norm, I've got to get drunk with you. Tonight. Good and drunk. You know what I mean?"

"We'll see."

As we rounded the corner, the squad car passed us from the opposite direction, sirens whining.

Neither of us spoke until I pulled up in front of Laurie's apartment. I patted Shannon's knee. "Sit tight. Be just a minute."

She didn't move, didn't open her eyes.

I reached the top step and pressed the buzzer, then leaned on it hard. Laurie's voice was wary, frightened. "Who is it?"

"Norm. Alone. Open up."

The door opened and I stepped inside.

"He's not here," Laurie said. "He just left."

I went into the bedroom. It was empty, as was the closet. On the table there were two half-filled coffee cups, still warm.

"So he left," I said harshly. "He's going to drive all the way to the county seat with one arm in a cast? Didn't we make a deal about Tuesday night? Bullock's troopers are combing the town for him right now."

Laurie's eyes were steady. "He can sue the city for false arrest."

I laughed. "We've got a dozen witnesses to swear he was drunk and disorderly, that he resisted arrest. My plans have changed. I'm not leaving town. Look, tell Matt when you see him that I'll give him five thousand dollars to forget all about that manila envelope."

"I'll tell him." Her voice was toneless. "But I know what his answer will be."

"All right." My patience was going. "Then he gets framed for that utilities shortage, tomorrow! Good night, Laurie."

I was halfway down the steps when she caught up with me. She was on the verge of tears.

"Please, Norm." She put one hand on my arm. "Don't do it to him. I'm begging you."

Shannon watched us from the Lincoln. Laurie gave her a long, searching look. "So she's the reason."

"Talk to Matt," I said. "Tell him he needs that envelope to substantiate any accusations. Tell him he's in no spot to bargain."

"All right." Laurie's lip trembled. "I'll call you later."

I slid behind the wheel of the Lincoln. "She seemed to have quite an affinity for you," Shannon said bitingly. "She's pretty."

"She hates my guts."

"Love and hate are both sides of the same coin. Don't lie to Shannon."

"I've got work to do tonight," I said irritably. "Our party will have to wait."

The quick intake of breath, the green eyes glowing. "What kind of work?"

"I've got to figure out how to dump Angelo tomorrow. And make a deal with my maniac brother."

"Then you won't mind if I take the car. The supermarket's open, and I've got shopping to do."

"Of course not. God, you're suspicious."

She dropped me at my apartment, and for just one moment her lean face was incredibly wistful as she kissed me good night. Her long body pressed against mine and her fingernails dug into the back of my neck. "It had better be business," she whispered fiercely. "I wanted you very badly tonight."

149

"There'll be other nights."

She smiled sweetly. Too sweetly.

The first thing I did was take a hot shower. Then I put on a bathrobe and slippers and poured myself a drink.

For the next hour I planned.

Tomorrow I would have Bullock liquidate Angelo. There would be some repercussions—perhaps a county probe— but that could all be handled. The important thing was to close down the poker parlors immediately, the cribs. Until after election. Oddly enough, I wasn't too worried about Matt. Laurie could reason with him. We would work out a deal.

The doorbell rang. Angelo?

I took Shannon's little automatic from my coat and slid the safety catch off. "Who is it?"

"Laurie. Alone." This was password night.

I opened the door. "Come in. Have a drink. Is he going to be reasonable?"

Laurie stepped inside. She wore a tan polo coat, and she was shivering.

"Soda, water, or neat?"

"No thanks." Her eyes darted about the room, taking in the blue leather couch, the gray carpeting. "Nice."

"You didn't come here to compliment me upon my interior decorating ability," I said dryly. "He's still stubborn?"

She nodded mutely. The lamplight struck sparks from her red-gold hair as she took off her coat I caught my breath. Her breasts looked full and defiant through the sheer dress.

"Nice outfit."

"I thought you'd like it."

Struck by a dark suspicion, I went to the window, peered down at Laurie's little yellow convertible sitting by the curb. It was empty. Her voice was tired, tinged with contempt. "Don't worry, I came alone."

"To tell me Matt's still going to play the fool?"

"To beg."

I stared at the proud gray eyes, the perfect body tensed and waiting.

I snickered. "Why do women think that's the ultimate solution? If all else fails, the bed is the last resort."

Laurie's face was pink. "Go home," I said. "It's a nice try, but it didn't come off."

The phone rang. It was Shannon.

"Darling, I can't sleep."

"You're not just checking?" I growled.

"Let me come over. Please. I bought some champagne—"

"Dammit, I'm busy."

Deliberately, Laurie laughed. Full throaty laughter tinged with malicious bitchery.

"Who's that?" Shannon asked tightly.

"It's just the radio. What's the matter with you?"

"I'm possessive."

The humming emptiness of the wire. I glared at Laurie.

"Tell me you're alone, darling. It's important to me."

"I'm alone."

"Good night," she said.

I hung up. "Damn you, Laurie. What were you trying to do?"

"She seems rather jealous," Laurie said thoughtfully.

"She's all woman. We're a team, partners in everything. And," I added brutally, "she's better in bed than you ever thought of being. Beat it."

Her head went back as if I'd slapped her, but the remark did not have the desired effect. She crossed to the sideboard and poured herself a stiff three fingers of rye. "You did offer me a drink?"

"Help yourself." I was getting nervous. I wanted her to leave.

"You're really going through with it, Norm? You're framing him?"

"No choice. He's a fanatic. Finish your drink and go home," I said, starting into the kitchen. I took my time putting a pot of coffee on the stove. There was silence from the living room. Then Laurie's voice.

"Perhaps I came here to prove something."

There was a silken rustling. I came out of the kitchen and stood transfixed.

Laurie was unbuttoning her blouse, shrugging it off her creamy shoulders, letting it drop to the rug. The skirt was next. Her gray eyes were enigmatic as she pulled her slip over her head. She stood wearing only black lace panties, bra, high heels and sheer hose. Desire smashed a velvet fist along my loins.

"To prove what?" My voice sounded thick.

"You said she was better."

Laurie calmly unhooked her bra, let it fall. There was a challenge in her face as she turned toward the bedroom. My throat was dry, my face hot. I followed her.

"You're trying to prove—"

152

"Don't talk," she said. "Don't say a word."

I put my hands on her shoulders, let them slide down to her hips. She was rigid as stone, eyes closed. Her arms came up and slid around my neck. I kissed her. Her lips were cold.

Then I heard the sound. The metallic click of a doorlatch sliding into place. Someone was in my apartment!

Laurie smiled. Her eyes opened and there was no passion there, only cold purpose.

"Who is it?" she called.

The sound of a door closing. Footsteps clicking hurriedly down the hall stairs.

I ran into the living room. It was empty. I threw open the door. The stairs were dark and deserted. From outside there was the cough of a motor, the scream of anguished tires clawing down the street. I got to the window just in time to see the Lincoln disappearing around the corner.

Laurie was dressing. I grabbed the telephone and frantically dialed Shannon's number. No answer. I hung up, then dialed again, waiting in an agony of suspense; then the slow, sick realization as I stared at Laurie's curling smile.

"You gambled," I said.

"I won."

"You would have gone through with it? Just on the chance she'd find us together?"

"She did find us together," Laurie said dreamily, "with my clothes scattered all over your living room."

I stared at her, slowly getting it.

Laurie was at the door. Something very close to pity was in her smile. "You see, Norm, I love Matt more than I hate you. And I hate you very much. It makes the difference."

153

She was gone. I started dialing again, counting the rings. I don't know how long I kept dialing.

XX

The alarm went off at seven. I lurched out of bed, head splitting, fumbling blindly for the button, whimpering little curses as the clock kept ringing. I smashed it against the floor and it was still.

Three cups of hot black coffee. Three cigarettes, brooding. The cold sting of the razor, the gray, nervous face in the mirror, the twitching mouth. Why had she stopped by last night? What if she went to Angelo, told him everything? For a moment I couldn't breathe.

I finished dressing and slipped Shannon's automatic into my coat pocket. I had to explain. She had to believe me. Shannon still had the Lincoln. I'd have to walk.

Ten blocks over to Olive Street. Ten blocks of feverish panting—the sweat running into my eyes—trying to think of some explanation that would satisfy her.

I unlocked Shannon's front door quietly with the duplicate key she'd given me. "Shannon," I called. "Honey, it's Norm!" Her bedroom was cold and still. The bed had not been slept in. I stared at it, empty and shaking.

I walked down Main and turned right on Center Street, past the closed bars, gray and ugly in the morning sunlight. I finally spotted the Lincoln, parked in front of the Golden Wheel. Angelo's hotel.

Rage pumped scaldingly into my throat. My fingers curled around the handle of the gun in my coat pocket.

She was in the back casino, at one of the crap tables. Her laughter was feverishly shrill as she threw the dice. She laughed wildly, blonde hair tossing, as the tired stickman placed more chips in front of her.

Angelo sat in a booth across the room, drinking coffee. He watched Shannon like a cat.

154

Shannon left the game, picked up her drink and wavered over to Angelo's table. Now they were talking. I walked toward them. Angelo's face was darkly impassive as he saw me. Shannon looked up with a distorted smile.

"Good morning, darling. Work hard last night?"

I caught her by the wrist, jerked her to her feet I slapped her openhanded, wanting to kill her.

"So we like to play," I said through my teeth. "Come on, you tramp, we're going home."

"Wait a minute." Angelo's cruel smile was etched with strain. "I got something to say."

"Say it!"

"You say Robin's okay?"

"That's right."

"Then you won't mind bringing me a letter from her? Today. Telling me how good she feels. You won't mind that?"

"No," I said, feeling the blood go out of my face.

"This afternoon, maybe? About four?"

"Sure," I said.

I dragged Shannon out through the lobby and threw her into the Lincoln. She was quiet, sullen. I drove in a cold rage, my thoughts spinning. Shannon nursed her wrist, swearing softly; then all at once she crumpled like a little girl and broke into a storm of weeping.

I pulled into her driveway and let her cry it out on my shoulder.

"Stop it," I said, putting an arm around her. "You won't believe this, but it's true. Listen."

I told her about Laurie, exactly the way it happened. She nodded

155

dully, but she didn't believe me. She would never believe me in a thousand years.

"When I saw her clothes in the living room I could have killed you," she breathed. "I went straight home and got some money. I felt hopped up, crazy. I gambled all night."

"What did you tell Angelo?"

"N-nothing," she sniffled. "He only asked me if Robin was all right. I played innocent, dumb."

Real dumb. Sure. I pictured the whispered hint to Angelo, the silken noose tightening about my throat. "We're leaving town," I told her. "Tonight. Get some sleep. Then get packed. How much you got left... two thousand, three?"

"I lost it all." Her eyes slid away from mine. "All of it, this morning. Does it matter, darling?"

I made myself kiss her. Under her tearful mask I could sense the squirming hate, the bitterness. Perhaps she did believe me. It didn't matter. Fear is the catalyst that turns love into hate, and I was very much afraid of her. There was no telling how much she had spilled to Angelo.

It was nine-thirty. The banks opened at ten. First I made myself stop at a downtown cafe and eat breakfast. The eggs felt slimy in my mouth and the coffee was like lye, but I got it down. By the time I reached the bank my nerves were screaming.

I drew out my entire account. Six thousand dollars. I tried to think of it as a real stake, a shining windfall for the poor slob who had hit town flat-broke less than a year ago, but it was nothing compared with what I might have in six months—if I stayed alive.

Driving to City Hall, I felt as if small, wild eyes were watching me. I kept searching the traffic for that prowling tan Mercury. I parked the Lincoln behind City Hall and went up to see Bullock.

"Any repercussions from last night?"

"Open and shut," Bullock said happily. "What's with Matt?"

"We'll have to smear him. Tell Kramer to wrap up Matt's ledger discrepancies this afternoon and get out a warrant. Alert the county attorney. Tell him Matt might make some wild accusations."

"Good idea. If we can just keep Angelo in line until after election..."

I laughed. The sound was indescribably vicious. It reminded me of Murdoch's laughter, ice splintering, things tearing apart. I began talking.

"You're raving!" Bullock whispered hoarsely. "You're demented, Sands. This town's ready to pop, right this minute. We don't dare smash Angelo yet—it'd be just what the opposition needs! They'd cry gang war, and they'd be right!"

"All right." I started for the door. "So long."

He sat frozen. "What are you going to do?"

"See the district attorney. A real fearless district attorney who eats crooked politicians for breakfast. I'll give him some reading matter. This afternoon he'll hit this town like a tornado. You might get off with five years, Tom."

"Goddammit," he yelled, "you're nuts! You're worse than Clem ever was. You're a stark, raving mad-dog crazy—"

I yanked him out of his chair and shook him till his teeth rattled. "You small-time yellow-livered bastard, by tonight Angelo will know I've crossed him. He'll tear this town apart! We've got to get him first. Angelo's mainstays are Froggy Martin and Spinelli. With the three of them gone, the rest will scatter like rats. I'll finger him for you, fair enough?"

All the fight was gone out of him. He took a deep breath and nodded. "All right. Where and when?"

I went over it with him for half an hour. The important part of it was timing.

An hour later I called Angelo at his hotel. "You'll get your letter this afternoon." I gave him Shannon's address. "See you at four o'clock sharp."

"She's all right? You haven't done nothing to her?"

"Oh, we cut off a few fingers to keep her in line—"

His frenzied roar again. I grinned into the mouthpiece, said, "Four sharp," and hung up.

Just enough to worry him. Enough to build up his strain to a howling crescendo of fear and worry. He was not yet sure if Robin was dead. Shannon was too smart to have given him more than a few bitter hints this morning. I could imagine the torment that was driving him mad right this minute.

I called Shannon.

"Norm, I'm worried."

"Don't be," I crooned into the phone. "I've stalled Angelo until midnight. But by then, honey, we'll be far away."

Even over the wire her contrition sounded real. "Darling, I'm sorry about this morning. Something bad's going to happen. I can feel it."

"I've got a few loose ends to tidy up," I said. "I'll pick you up at five sharp. I'll have twelve grand in my jeans."

The money, of course, was the bait. She'd wait for me all afternoon. But she'd get—Angelo.

The shock would snap Shannon into a hysterical confession. Angelo would probably kill her.- At ten minutes after four Bullock's troopers would arrive in a prowl car. Angelo would be killed resisting arrest. Everything dovetailed. No loose ends.

The warrant for Matt was already out. By midnight he'd be behind bars. I felt like a heel, but what the hell, I told myself, it was his own stubborn fault.

It was twelve-thirty when I drove out of the service station. The Lincoln was oiled and gassed. The motor purred eagerly as I passed

Orange Street and hit the main highway. The speedometer shot up to eighty and hung there quivering. Five miles then ten toward the coast and Highway 101. At first I kept glancing into the rearview mirror, but there was no sign of that tan Mercury and the highway was a smoking white ribbon of empty concrete. I leaned back and lit a cigarette. The relief was invigorating. Tonight I'd phone Bullock from Los Angeles, perhaps even Vegas, to find out how things had gone. In any case, I'd take a two-week vacation. Perhaps Catalina. Fishing, sleeping in the sun. I had six thousand dollars, and after election there would be more, much more. I began whistling.

It was too bad about Shannon. I would have a few bad nights, but I was used to bad nights. Thirty miles, forty. The jeweled beach towns rushing past; Dana Point, Newport, Laguna. A wicked little thought nibbled at my brain. I had forgotten something ...

I was coming into Laguna when the thought suddenly uncoiled. I slammed on the brakes and sat fighting panic, coldly weighing my chances.

It was only one-fifteen. There was still time. Time enough to make a squealing U-turn, to roar back along the highway, doing ninety now and slowing down to sixty for the beach towns, swearing at the red lights. Just the other side of Dana Point I ran a stop sign, and there was the strident blare of a siren. He pulled me over to the side of the road and took an eternity getting off his motorcycle, the way they always do.

"Kind of hitting it up back there, weren't you?"

"Look, write it up and spare the sermon," I snapped. "I haven't got all day."

That was a mistake. His youngish face hardened. "Operator's license!"

He took ten whole minutes to write that ticket. All the time I sat fuming, trying to keep from letting the rage show. Calling myself nineteen kinds of a fool for not remembering that manila envelope in Shannon's refrigerator. Sweat broke out on my face as the picture unfolded:

Shannon realizing she'd been set up for the patsy; Angelo going berserk with fury; Shannon offering him the records, trying to make a deal, telling him everything. Angelo would kill her anyway—I knew that. But now he'd have the records. And he'd know how to use them.

When I finally drove away, that cop followed me. He followed me for five miles. Carefully, I kept it under forty, raging inside, feeling that gun in my coat, wanting to use it.

Finally, when I turned left on the inland route, he kept going and didn't turn off after me. I made the next twenty miles in twelve minutes flat. It was ten after three when I careened into Shannon's driveway. I ran up the steps and threw open the front door.

"Come in," Matt said. He held the gun pointed carefully at my navel. "We've been waiting."

XXI

Matt stood in the middle of the living room, smiling crookedly. His left arm was still in the plaster cast, but the gun in his right hand was steady. Shannon sat limply on the sofa. "He's crazy," she whispered. "He keeps asking for—"

"The records," Matt broke in. "Where are they?"

I walked toward him confidently, my hand outstretched. "Give it here, Galahad. It's not loaded, remember?"

"I'm warning you, Norm."

I threw back my head to laugh and Matt pistol-whipped me across the jaw. The pain was blinding. My brother Matt? For a second I couldn't believe it. It was like being attacked by a rabbit. Then rage choked me and I went for him. This time the barrel smashed against my temple.

"You bastard," I said incredulously. I was on hands and knees, watching my blood drip down in tiny red spots on the carpet. I got up slowly.

Matt's face was contorted with emotion. "I'm not your brother any more. Just a stranger who's going to kill you. Unless you deliver, right this minute."

I touched my cheek and stared at my red fingers. This wasn't really happening! I said, dreamily, "They're in a safe-deposit box."

"Where's the key?"

"I don't have it with me."

The gun smashed into my mouth this time. I stood reeling, tasting iron and salty blood. Shannon flew at him with a wordless cry and Matt shoved her hard against the piano. I shivered with fury as I reached in my coat pocket, but I made it look like I was trembling with fear.

"Here," I muttered. "Take it." My fingers touched the cold steel of Shannon's automatic. "How was I to know you meant bus—"

My right hand was a snake striking, and there was the ugly crunch of metal on bone. Matt's gun thumped on the carpet. He stared stupidly at his numb wrist, at me.

"Now," I said grinning, "you're going to—"

Agony exploded whitely in my groin and flared up to the top of my skull. I lay on my side, huddled into a moaning ball of pain. He had given me the knee! His own brother! I was clawing for the gun, and Matt's shoe was swinging at my face. Then the last fragments of light splintered into darkness.

"Darling? Oh Norm, are you all right?"

The genuine misery in her voice. The cold cloth on my forehead.

"Where is he?" I mumbled through puffed lips.

"Lie quietly, darling, please." She was crying, kneeling over me with a wet washcloth, and crying. "He's gone. I gave them to him, those damned records. He would have killed you."

"You gave them to him?" I struggled to my feet, shaking. The room

161

spun. I wanted to hit her, but I was too weak. I slumped to my knees. "What time is it?" I croaked.

"Three forty-five." Her voice shook. "Oh sweetheart—"

"Oh sweetheart," I mimicked spitefully. "I'm a jealous woman, but I love you. I love you so much I'll give Matt the ammunition to kill you. I'll tell Angelo that Robin's dead, darling, just to teach you not to sleep with another woman!" Hatred throttled me as I tried to rise. At last I lay, cursing her weakly. "Got to get out of here," I said. "Help me up."

As she helped me to the sofa, there was the grinding of brakes outside. Then, heavy feet coming up the walk.

"Who's there?" Shannon called.

"Shut up," I whispered. I got to my feet. Nausea stirred blackly in my stomach. The tiny automatic lay in a corner. As I picked it up, the knocking at the door became loud, angry.

"Stall him," I whispered. "No matter what happens, stall him! You got that?"

She was breathless with panic, but she nodded. I took her gently by the shoulders, pulled her against me. The knocking was thunder. "I love you," I said, meaning it. "If we come out of this I'll make it up to you." I kissed her. "Answer it."

I made it to the bedroom closet just as the front door opened.

"We're a little early." Angelo's bass rumble. "I got impatient. You mind?"

Shannon's frightened "no."

It was dark and close in the closet. Silk things rustled as I moved. Silk things that whispered of Shannon, that smelled of her—a clean, April-rain freshness. Realization came over me in a burst of grief and bitterness. God help me, I loved her.

I opened the closet door just a hair. I could see Angelo's knees in the angle the hall made with the living room.

162

"... some coffee?" Shannon was saying.

"Sure." Froggy Martin's thin voice. "Don't mind if we do."

"No coffee," Angelo said. "This ain't a social call. When's he coming?"

Shannon, brightly, "Norm? Oh, he'll be hours."

"He better be minutes. Where's Robin?"

"I—don't know."

The seconds dragged by like years. My insides felt smashed. I wondered if Matt had continued kicking me when I was out. Sir Galahad with a gun. I felt a queer, perverse pride in him.

"It's four o'clock." Spinelli's voice.

"Give him time," Angelo said.

I breathed shallowly.

"I'll make some coffee," Shannon said.

"You just sit." Angelo's voice was animal now, the thin veneer of civilization peeling away as the minutes passed.

It must be four-ten by now, I thought. Bullock would come soon. He had to come!

Silence from the living room. Then Froggy's nasal whine. "He's not coming! Look at her, Angelo, look how white she is. He's not coming and you been played for a sucker. It's some kind of trap, I can feel it!"

Suddenly Angelo went mad. "Damn you," he blazed. "When's he coming? Is this another of his stinking blind alleys? Is it?"

Shannon sounded hysterical. "He'll be here later—"

The sound of a slap. Her muffled sob.

"You were in on that snatch," Angelo grated. "Where is she?"

"Honestly, I don't kn—"

The slaps continued. Angelo's laughter, merciless as flint. Goddamn him, if he hit her again, I'd blow his brains through the back of his head! Where was Bullock?

I ground my fists into my ears, breathing over and over like a litany, "I'll make it up to you," but I could still hear those sounds. Sounds of a dress tearing. The creaking of sofa springs. Shannon's little cries. Spinelli's lascivious titter. "Stall them," I had told her. She'd stall them with her body, with death if necessary. Because she loved me. The thought was a searing coal.

"I'll show you," Shannon said in a tortured whisper. "Please stop. I'll show you where she is."

"That's better. Real better. Let's go."

I couldn't take it any more. A tiny corner of my mind was cold, infinitely scornful, telling me I couldn't afford luxuries like passion or revenge. Just wait. Let them go for the time being.

But I slid the closet door open and sighted on Angelo's right knee, all that was visible of him. I pressed the trigger.

The spiteful crack of the .22 in the closet was deafening. Angelo went down like an eyelid and Froggy dived for the protection of the sofa. I reached the hall door firing wildly.

Shep Spinelli was crouched in the center of the room, shooting into the hallway. Wood fragments dissolved next to my cheek as I fired two quick shots at him. His hands flew to his throat. He was flopping on the carpet as I stepped full into the living room, a perfect target I shot at Angelo three times. He rolled frantically for cover as my bullets hit the carpet next to him.

Froggy's white face was a blur behind the sofa. I wheeled toward him as a firecracker went off in my chest. The room tilted crazily and the carpet jumped up to hit me in the face.

Stillness. I coughed, feeling the blood in my throat, thick and warm.

164

Froggy stood up, spraddle-legged. His eyes were bright. He took careful aim at my head. Angelo's bellow stopped him.

"I want him alive." Angelo's voice was thick with agony. "God, my knee. I think he smashed the kneecap."

Shannon lay half-across the sofa. Her eyes were closed. A crimson line trickled down from the corner of her mouth.

"Where's Robin?" Angelo said.

"She's dead," I answered dully.

"You're a liar!" He wouldn't believe it. He hobbled to his feet, swaying. "Ask the girl, Froggy."

Froggy was shaking her. She whimpered. Her fingers moved. "Norm," she murmured.

I crawled across the carpet toward her.

"Where's Robin?" Froggy said.

Shannon's lips moved. "Norm?" she breathed. "Darling?"

"Right here." I cradled her head in my arms. "Tell them about Robin, honey."

"She's fine." Shannon's smile was drowsy. "Isn't that right, darling? Is it over at last, darling, all over? Can we go now? Can we see Paris?"

"We'll see Paris." My eyes were stinging. It was hard to see.

"Just us," she said. "The Riviera..."

Her head drooped sideways. She was smiling, but she wasn't breathing.

"Take him," Angelo said.

Froggy threw my right arm over his shoulder. They took me outside, put me in the back seat of the Buick. My chest hurt. I kept coughing, a bubbling cough. I tried to tell them about Robin.

Angelo's laughter was insane. "She said Robin was fine. I heard her say it. The last thing she said. You'll show us where Robin is."

"We got ways," Froggy said.

I tried to laugh, and it came out a sob.

The snarl of the siren behind us. Angelo swore and gunned the Buick. The squad car came hurtling alongside the Buick, forcing it toward the curb. Angelo was fighting the wheel, cursing gutturally. I tried to yell at the squad car, to tell Bullock he was too late, and a bullet frosted the window, spraying my face with glass.

The whole squad car was squirting flame. Froggy was leaning past Angelo, firing; then all at once his face seemed to dissolve in a red smear. He disappeared behind the front seat. As we careened around the corner, the Buick swerved into the squad car and I slammed hard against the left door. The squad car teetered sideways and smashed into a telephone pole in a jumble of glass and sound. My chest was ripping apart. The last thing I heard was Angelo's metallic laughter.

XXII

An eternity of pain-racked blackness. Blackness and time and agony.

The room was small, incredibly dirty. Leprous patches of plaster flaked the walls and ceiling. A grimy window showed pale daylight outside. I moved my head and saw the battered table, the rickety chair. Angelo was slumped over the table, his head buried in his arms.

I tried to move. My straw pallet rustled beneath me. Angelo's head lifted. His face was something out of a sick dream—the grinning mouth, the black eyes sunken and mad. He reeled to his feet, clutching the table for support.

"Where are we?" My chest throbbed horribly. It hurt to talk.

"Holed up on Orange Street," Angelo said. "This is the third day." He lit a cigarette. "You're tough, baby. That's good. Where's Robin?" I tried to tell him, but he wouldn't believe me. He would never believe me. He had an obsession that Robin was alive and safe.

He told me the news, leering. How the whole town had gone smash. The mayor and half the city council had resigned. The county attorney's boys had closed down the cribs and most of the bars. Bullock had been killed in the squad car smashup. Angelo's boys had all fled.

"Rats," Angelo said, "deserting a sinking ship. They wanted me to come, too. They wouldn't help me find Robin. But you'll help me, baby. Where is she? Where's Robin?"

"She's dead."

"Come off it." The black eyes gleamed with a cunning madness. "You got a price, I got money. I got something else, too."

Angelo hobbled over to me. Deliberately, he snuffed out his cigarette on my cheek. I tried to scream and my chest was a crater of red fire. I passed out.

Voices penetrated the pain. A strange voice, dignified and tired. "Senor, I cannot be responsible. You must have an operation immediately. Your leg—"

"Never mind my leg. You get paid to answer questions and keep your mouth shut. What about him?"

The doctor leaned over me. He had kind brown eyes and a straggly white goatee. His fingers probed. "Shock. Loss of blood. As I told you yesterday, he needs plasma. But I think you, my friend, have gangrene."

"It's just a scratch. You croakers are all alike." Angelo's grin was feverish. He hobbled to the table, ripped open the sack of hamburgers and fries, began to wolf them down. "Only trouble is, it stinks. Better leave some more iodine."

I saw his leg, the trouser ripped away from it at the knee. The

167

makeshift bandage, caked with blood and filthy. The ugly purple-green swelling. The smell.

"Same time tomorrow, doc?"

"As you wish." The doctor folded his stethoscope precisely and picked up his black bag with a shrug of resignation. Angelo came over to my pallet, his grin hungry, expectant. "He's well enough to talk?"

"He has the constitution of a bull, that one. He will live to be ninety."

Angelo threw back his head and laughed.

THE END

www.ingramcontent.com/pod-product-compliance
Lightning Source LLC
Chambersburg PA
CBHW020245150626
46552CB00020B/386